CONTENTS

CHAPTER ONE

A DAY LIKE NO OTHER

The sun peeked through the leaves of Rosewood Forest, casting dappled shadows on the ground. On the edge of the forest, nestled in a cozy house with blue shutters and a red door, the Pinkfish family was just waking up to another Sunday.

Elena and Mira, the spirited twins, bounded down the stairs two at a time, their laughter ringing like chimes. Their fluffy white cat, Snowball, sat at the bottom of the stairs, tail twitching as if he knew a great adventure was about to unfold.

"First one to the kitchen gets the last chocolate chip pancake!" Elena called, sprinting ahead. Mira, always up for a challenge, raced after her, their matching braids flying behind them.

In the kitchen, their mom, Maya, was flipping pancakes with one hand while checking her notebook with the other. She was a journalist, often on the lookout for the next big news story, but today was all about family.

"Smells amazing, Mom!" Elena said, sliding into her chair.

Derek, their dad, entered with a thick book tucked under his arm, excitement radiating from him. "You'll never believe what I found out about the bioluminescent fungi in the forest!" he exclaimed, adjusting his glasses.

Elena and Mira exchanged curious glances. "Are we going into the forest today?" Elena asked, her fork poised mid-air.

"Not today, but we have a fun family project!" Derek replied, placing his book on the table. "We're going to build a birdhouse for the backyard."

"Can we decorate it?" Mira asked, her eyes lighting up.

"Absolutely!" Maya said. "I brought some paints and stickers. Let's make it the most colorful birdhouse in Rosewood!"

After breakfast, the twins headed outside, Snowball trailing behind, curious about the commotion. They gathered supplies from the garage: wood planks, nails, and the brightest paint colors they could find.

As they worked together, laughter echoed through the yard. "This will be the best birdhouse ever!" Elena declared, painting swirls of blue and green.

Mira concentrated on painting flowers, her creativity flowing freely. "I hope we get all kinds of birds! Maybe even a bluebird!"

"Or a robin!" Elena chimed in. "What if we attract something magical?" The twins giggled at the thought of magical birds.

Just then, Maya called from the porch, "Don't forget to leave some space for the entrance!"

But unbeknownst to the family, a secret was brewing in the hidden depths of Rosewood Forest.

Somewhere deep within the woods where no human set their foot, an ancient oak tree twisted toward the sky, its gnarled branches shrouded in mist. Hidden among the roots, a peculiar figure worked tirelessly—a witch, her wild hair tangled with leaves and her cloak a patchwork of colors that blended into the forest.

The witch, squinted at a bubbling cauldron, murmuring incantations while stirring a glowing green liquid. She paused, glancing around, and picked up a tiny seed from the ground. With a flick of her wrist, she poured the glowing potion onto the seed and planted it in the rich soil.

The air shimmered with energy as the ground trembled slightly. Within moments, the seed began to sprout, roots twisting and reaching toward the earth. A trunk shot up, growing taller and taller until it burst into a magnificent tree. Its branches unfurled, and soon, bright yellow fruits dangled like tiny suns, glowing against the green backdrop of the forest.

"Perfect!" she cackled, her eyes sparkling with delight.

Back at the Pinkfish home, the twins were finishing up their birdhouse, covered in paint splotches and giggles. "It looks fantastic!" Derek said, stepping back to admire their handiwork. "Let's let it dry and see if we can hang it up later."

"Can we go for a walk later, too?" Mira asked, looking toward the inviting woods.

"Of course! Just a quick one," Maya replied, ruffling their hair. "We'll check the birdhouse and see if any feathered friends have come by."

With their project complete, the family settled on the porch with a pitcher of lemonade. They watched the sky turn shades of orange and pink as the sun dipped lower, content in each other's company.

In the warm light of their room, Elena and Mira were buzzing with excitement as they prepared for their school trip to the archaeology site the next day. They spread maps and brochures across the floor, eagerly discussing all the fascinating things they hoped to see.

"I can't believe we're finally going on this trip!" Mira exclaimed, her eyes sparkling with enthusiasm.

Elena grinned. "And ancient artifacts! This is going to be the best experience ever!"

As they packed their backpacks, they wanted to make their trip extra special. "Let's write down our wishes for the adventure!" Mira suggested, and Elena nodded eagerly.

They grabbed colorful paper and pens, pouring their hopes into small chits. Elena wrote, "May we discover something amazing!" while Mira scribbled, "Let's make unforgettable memories!"

With a sense of anticipation, they sealed their wishes in a small envelope and tucked it safely in Elena's backpack. "Tomorrow is going to be incredible!" Mira declared, and as they settled into bed, they drifted off to sleep, dreaming of the archaeological wonders that awaited them.

CHAPTER TWO

A DREAMER'S WAKE UP CALL

The very next morning, Mira was lost in a vivid dream where she received a letter from Hogwarts School of Witchcraft and Wizardry. The dream was so real that she could almost feel the parchment in her hands.

Suddenly, a voice pierced through the dream: "Wake up, wake up!"

Mira groggily opened her eyes to see her twin sister, Elena, standing beside her bed, already dressed in her school uniform. Elena tapped her foot and frowned, "I'm going to be late for school, thanks to you" Elena scolded. "You have five minutes to get ready. Did you forget we have a school trip today?"

Mira blinked in surprise, her dream quickly fading as the reality of Elena's words sank in. She squinted at her sister, her vision still hazy, she slowly rubbed her eyes. Now she could see the frustrated expression of her sister and sprang out of bed, hurriedly getting dressed.

Though they were twins, the two couldn't have been more different. Elena, older by a mere five minutes, was the responsible, practical one, always focused and punctual. She loved organizing things and making sure everything was just right. Mira, on the other hand, was the dreamy and imaginative, her head often lost in the clouds, filled with magical stories and fantastic ideas or in this case, in the magical corridors of Hogwarts. Elena and Mira were both sleek and stylish in their own ways. Mira's wavy hair framed her face with a wild, textured charm, while Elena's straight hair fell smoothly and neatly around her shoulders.

Elena's practicality serves as a stabilizing force for Mira's flights of fancy, helping to transform her imaginative dreams into tangible, achievable plans. When Mira dreams up fantastical ideas, like secret fairy gardens or magical pathways, Elena takes the dreams and figures out how to make them real. She creates detailed plans, organizes the necessary materials, and ensures everything fits together smoothly. In this way Elena's practical approach grounds Mira's creativity turning abstract concepts into concrete projects.

On the flip side, Mira's creativity inspires Elena to think beyond the ordinary. Mira's whimsical ideas and colorful visions encourage Elena to stretch her imagination and consider possibilities she might not have thought of her own. By seeing the world through Mira's imaginative lens, Elena learns to embrace new perspectives and explore creative solutions. Together, their unique strength blends seamlessly, allowing them to create something that is both well-organized and magically enchanting. Once, Mira mentioned how wonderful it would be to attend a school like Hogwarts, where students are sorted into different houses by a sorting hat. Inspired by this idea, Elena collaborated with her parents to create a sorting hat. The school embraced the concept and sorted everyone into various houses, organizing sports and cultural competitions between them. It turned out to be an incredibly fun day, with the entire school applauding both Elena and Mira for their brilliant idea.

"Girls, breakfast is ready!" Maya called from downstairs. Mira and Elena quickly grabbed their bags and dashed downstairs to join their parents at the table. Mira and Elena quickly grabbed their lunch boxes and a slice of bread before dashing out the door to catch the school bus. In their hurry, they almost tripped over Snowball, the cat, who had just finished her playtime chasing birds.

"They never eat their breakfast," Derek muttered with a sigh as Maya called after them, "Don't forget your water bottles!" But the girls were already gone. After finishing their breakfast, Derek and Maya reflected on how their lives had intertwined in unexpected ways.

Derek's love for inventive projects had led him to create the Chipmunks Premier League, where a group of chipmunks faced a series of challenges he'd designed to win a box of nuts. The videos of this quirky idea went viral, catching the attention of Maya, who came to interview Derek about his amusing concept. Their shared enthusiasm and mutual respect blossomed into love, leading them to marry and start a family. And so, Mira and Elena came into the world, embodying the creative spirit of their parents.

"Can you believe how fast they're growing up?" Maya mused.

"Every day is an adventure with them," Derek replied, a smile spreading across his face.

Derek and Maya waved goodbye and hurried off to their respective jobs. With their departure, the once bustling house fell into a peaceful silence.

CHAPTER THREE

PATH TO THE ANCIENT DISCOVERY

Elena and Mira sprinted down the street, barely making it onto the school bus just as the doors swung shut behind them. "Late as usual, I won't wait for you the next time!" grumbled the old bus driver. "It won't happen again, Sir!" Elena replied, giving her sister a pointed look. They rushed to join the rest of the sixth graders.

The bus was bustling with kids of all ages. Younger children sat near the front, chatting excitedly or giggling with friends, while older students occupied the back seats, some chatting quietly and others absorbed in their books. The bus was a lively mix of energy and noise, with groups of friends catching up and sharing stories. Despite the commotion, everyone followed basic safety rules—like sitting down while the bus was moving and keeping their voices down. It was a colorful snapshot of the school day, full of friendship and youthful excitement.

(Fun fact: Ever wondered why school buses are painted yellow? It's for safety reasons. The bright yellow color is highly visible in various weather conditions, such as fog or rain, making the bus stand out to other drivers.)

Elena and Mira attended Neev Academy, chosen by their parents for its bright, modern classrooms and safe outdoor play areas. The caring teachers used creative methods to engage students, ensuring everyone felt happy and supported while encouraged to do their best.

Once Elena and Mira arrived at school, their class teacher was already waiting for them. A few students were running and playing around Ms. Sumaya, who was everyone's favorite. Known for her kindness and warmth, Ms. Sumaya taught Science and was loved by all. Many students tried their hardest to earn top marks, hoping to make a good impression on her. However, Ms. Sumaya was never partial; she cherished all her students equally and encouraged each one to do their best. Standing around 5'2 feet tall, Ms. Sumaya's height was a point of excitement for the kids, who were thrilled to see how they had grown to be as tall as their beloved teacher.

Once all the students who had signed up for the field trip arrived, Ms. Sumaya gathered them to give instructions. The class fell into silence.

Safety First:

- Stay together: Don't wander off alone.

- Be aware of your surroundings: Look out for potential hazards.

- Follow the rules: Always listen to your teachers and chaperones.

Respectful Behavior:

- Be considerate: Respect the environment and the people around you.

- Follow local rules: Adhere to any specific regulations or guidelines.

- Be polite: Use good manners and be courteous to everyone.

Emergency Procedures:

- Know the contact information: Have emergency numbers readily available.

- Follow instructions: In case of an emergency, listen to your teachers and follow their guidance.

Ms. Sumaya looked at her silent students and said, "Last but not least, have fun, make the most of your outing, and create positive memories." As soon as she finished speaking, the students burst into laughter and started chatting excitedly.

The class was divided into groups of three, and Mira and Elena were joined by Xavier. Xavier, a shy boy, lived with his mother, a fashion designer. His father had passed away recently due to an illness, and he missed him deeply every day. Mira and Elena were aware of Xavier's situation and had shown kindness and extended their friendship when he and his mother had moved into their neighborhood. Their support had helped Xavier feel more welcomed and included. The trio settled into their seats on the bus as it set off for their destination.

The school was taking them to a recently discovered archaeological marvel, a trip made possible by the government's initiative to inspire students by connecting them with history. The outing aimed to spark curiosity and appreciation for the past, giving the younger generation a unique learning experience.

As the school bus rumbled down the road, the excited chatter of the sixth graders filled the air. It had been a long time since their last trip, and the kids were eager for a bit of fun.

Whenever a pedestrian walked by, they gleefully tossed their notes into the air, shouting, "Wish us luck!" Their laughter echoed down the street, each flying chit carrying their hopes and excitement for the journey ahead. It felt like a celebration of the adventure that awaited them, each shout mingling with the soft rustle of the notes as they danced in the breeze.

Amidst their joyful chaos, Ms. Sumaya seized the moment to keep the energy high. "Alright, everyone! How about a game of 'I Spy'?" she suggested, her eyes sparkling with enthusiasm. The kids perked up, eager for a fun distraction.

Ms. Sumaya: "Alright, everyone, let's play a game of 'I Spy' to pass the time. I'll start us off. Ready?"

The kids cheered, their faces lighting up with anticipation.

Ms. Sumaya: "I spy with my little eye something that is... green."

Lily: "The trees! Are you spying on the trees?"

Ms. Sumaya: "Good guess, but no, it's not the trees."

Jake: "The grass! The grass outside the window?"

Ms. Sumaya: "Nope, not the grass."

The kids looked around, scanning the bus and the scenery outside. Meanwhile, Elena, sitting by the window, spotted something.

Elena: "Is it the green backpack on the seat in front of me?"

Ms. Sumaya: "Yes, that's it! Nice job, Elena."

The kids cheered, and Ms. Sumaya smiled. Now it was Lily's turn to spy something.

Lily: "Okay, I spy with my little eye something that is... blue."

Anna: "The sky?"

Lily: "Nope, not the sky."

Omar: "The blue sign over there!"

Lily: "Nope, not the sign. But you're on the right track!"

Aadya: "The blue seatbelt?"

Lily: "Yes, that's right! The blue seatbelt in the front row."

Jake: "I spy with my little eye something that is... dreaming."

Everyone: "Mira!!"

The bus was filled with delighted giggles and high-fives as the kids guessed the answers. Mira, who had been gazing out the window and lost in her dreams, snapped back to reality, scratching her head in confusion. Xavier, seated beside her, smiled and explained that they were playing the "I Spy" game. Mira quickly joined in, and the game continued with each child taking their turn. The bus ride turned into a lively and joyful adventure.

After thirty minutes of playing "I Spy," Ms. Sumaya noticed that the kids were starting to lose interest as they ran out of things to spot. She announced, "Alright, let's switch things up and play a Story Chain game. One person will start a story with a single sentence, and then the next person will add another sentence, and so on. We'll create a collaborative story together."

The game began with Ms Sumaya starting a story with a simple sentence.

Ms. Sumaya: "Once upon a time, in a land where the sun never set..."

She began. The next student in the row picked up where she left off, adding their own twist.

Jake: "There lived a brave knight who wanted to find a magical treasure hidden deep in the forest."

The story continued to weave through the bus, with each student adding their own unique line.

Omar: "The knight set out on his quest with a talking cat as his companion,"

Another student chimed in, followed by someone else adding:

Mira: "They faced a dragon guarding the entrance to a secret cave."

Elena: "The dragon, with scales that shined like precious gems, roared as the knight and his talking cat approached."

Lily: "The dragon, instead of initiating a fight, presented a challenge. 'Solve my riddle, and I shall let you pass,' the dragon said. 'I'm full of keys but open no doors. What am I?'"

Max: "The knight and the cat pondered the riddle intensely."

After a moment, Max turned to Lily and asked, "Do you know the answer?" With a thoughtful look, Lily replied, "The answer is a piano."

Max: "The knight and the cat nodded in understanding. The cat meowed, 'A piano!'"

Aadya: "You have answered correctly. The treasure is hidden behind this cave's waterfall."

Anna: "Behind a sparkling waterfall, they found a chest and returned home with it."

Ms. Sumaya: "Inside, they discovered not gold, but a map to the treasure."

Ms. Sumaya brought the story back to life. Laughter and enthusiastic chatter filled the bus as the story grew more imaginative and wild with each new contribution. Characters encountered talking trees, mysterious potions, and enchanted creatures. By the time the bus reached their destination, the story had become an epic adventure filled with twists and turns that made everyone eager to hear the final outcome. The game not only passed the time but also sparked creativity and team spirit among the students, setting a positive tone for the rest of their exciting day.

As the bus neared the archaeological site, the game wrapped up amid laughter and excitement. The sixth graders had a blast, and what initially seemed like a long journey had transformed into a ride filled with smiles and cherished memories. Ms. Sumaya and the kids shared a satisfied feeling, knowing they had set a fun tone for the trip.

CHAPTER FOUR

THE DOG AND THE ASTRONOMERS

Once everyone arrived closer to the archaeological site, Ms. Sumaya gathered the students and addressed them.

"Students, to reach the site, we need to trek for 30 minutes. Please carry only essentials such as food, water, and a first aid kit, and avoid bringing anything heavy," Ms. Sumaya instructed. The students nodded in agreement and began their trek up the hill.

Elena sighed in relief. "Thank goodness Mom called and reminded Ms Sumaya to give us the water bottles. It would have been tough to hike without water." Mira nodded in agreement, grateful for her mother's foresight.

As the students embarked on their trek up the hill toward the archaeological site, they were immersed in a rich tapestry of natural beauty and sensory experiences. The trail was adorned with vibrant wildflowers and dense greenery, creating a colorful and inviting atmosphere. Along the way, the students glimpsed various wildlife, from chirping birds flickering through the trees to small mammals scurrying across the path. Excitement surged when Aadya, one of the students, spotted a graceful deer peeking through the bush, it added an unexpected thrill to their journey. Intriguing rock formations and geological features emerged, telling the story of the area's natural history. Informative trail markers and signs provided valuable insights, offering context about the local environment and the archaeological site they were approaching. The fresh, crisp air was energizing, while the gentle sounds of rustling leaves and distant streams created a calming, immersive experience. Together, these elements made the trek both a visual feast and an educational adventure, enhancing the students anticipation for the site ahead.

Ms. Sumaya, leading the way at the front with a map in hand, was accompanied by a few other teachers who stayed in the middle and at the back to ensure the students safety. As the students moved in their designated groups, Elena, Mira, and Xavier sprinted ahead and joined Ms. Sumaya. Elena, eager to learn, asked, "Miss, can you please tell us more about this site? We want to understand it better so we know what to look out for when we get there."

Ms. Sumaya smiled and nodded. "Of course! This archaeological site is quite fascinating. It dates back over 300 years and It is a unique structure , which is unlike anything that is seen before and it was discovered only recently. The site includes ancient ruins that reveal a lot about the people who lived here long ago. You'll see old structures and artifacts that tell stories about their daily lives, beliefs, and culture."

She continued, "As you explore, pay attention to the different types of artifacts and their placement. Each piece offers clues about how these people used to live. Remember to respect the site—avoid touching or disturbing the artifacts, and follow the guidelines provided by our guides."

"Also," she added, "be on the lookout for informative signs that explain the significance of different areas. They will help you understand what you're seeing and why it's important. Enjoy the adventure and keep your eyes open for interesting details!"

"Let me also tell you guys How it was discovered."

"Okay" Miss, said Xavier.

Ms. Sumaya continued, "Not long ago, space agencies predicted a spectacular meteor shower, and a group of astronomy enthusiasts came to this very place for stargazing. They trekked up the hill just as we are doing now. At the top, there is a cave, and the astronomers set up their observation spot at the cave's entrance to watch the sky. In places with less light pollution, like this cave, you can see the night sky much clearer."

She paused for a moment, then added, "The city lights and dust make it hard to see many stars, which is why they chose this location. Now, here's something interesting: they had brought their pet dog along with them. While they were set up at the cave entrance, the dog began sniffing around inside the cave. After a while, one of the astronomers noticed the dog was missing. They were certain it had gone into the cave."

Ms. Sumaya's voice grew more mysterious. "They carefully examined the cave and discovered that, in one corner, thick bushes had grown. After clearing the bushes, they found a hidden hole in the wall. If you looked closely, you could see the faint outline of a door that had been carefully concealed. It seemed like a recent earthquake had dislodged a stone, revealing the hidden entrance. They called for their dog and heard barking coming from behind the wall, but the dog did not return. Worried and with it being late and dark, they decided to wait until morning to investigate further. They settled into their sleeping bags after dinner.

In the early morning, one of the astronomers awoke to a strange sensation on his face. Opening his eyes, he was relieved to see the missing dog nestled beside him. Everyone was overjoyed to have the dog back, but their curiosity about the mysterious door in the cave grew stronger. They were convinced that the hole in the wall was more than it seemed and that the dog had somehow been inside it.

Determined to uncover the mystery, they decided to seek help from the local villagers. However, many of the older villagers were reluctant to assist, as they recalled eerie stories passed down through generations about the cave. Although nothing untoward had happened in the last century, the recent discovery of the hidden door had reignited old fears. Despite this, a few brave young villagers agreed to join the explorers.

When they reached the cave, the group cleared away the debris from the door. Despite their efforts, none of the villagers were willing to venture inside. So, the original group proceeded. Inside, they found ancient inscriptions and idols, as well as a narrow passage that could accommodate an average-sized adult. They ventured into the passage and soon realized it was a labyrinth, with walls appearing at every turn. To avoid getting lost, they marked their path as they explored.

Eventually, they stumbled upon several small, house-like structures within the maze. Upon returning, they reported their findings to the government. Archaeologists were dispatched to conduct an initial investigation, confirming the site's historical significance. For now, only students are permitted to visit, and the site remains closed to the general public while further research continues."

The trio found the story incredibly captivating, and by the time Ms. Sumaya finished recounting it, their mouths were agape in astonishment. Xavier was so engrossed that he nearly had a fly buzz into his mouth, barely noticing as he stared wide-eyed at Ms. Sumaya, completely absorbed in the thrilling tale.

"But Miss, what if we get lost"? asked Mira, scared.

Ms. Sumaya reassured them with a smile, "Don't worry, they've marked the path, so as long as we stay on it, we won't get lost. I'll be with you the entire time to make sure everything goes smoothly."

The trio sighed in relief, feeling a weight lift off their shoulders. They hadn't realized they had been trekking for nearly 30 minutes, and when they finally reached the hilltop, they were greeted by the archaeological site. The archaeologists instructed them not to touch anything and handed out shoe covers to ensure the site remained clean and undisturbed.

CHAPTER FIVE

A SPARK OF A NEW ADVENTURE

As the students stepped into the cave, their eyes grew wide with excitement, and their mouths dropped open in awe. The cave matched exactly what Ms. Sumaya had described. In one of the hidden corners, they discovered a door that was cleverly hidden and hard to spot, now had an opening big enough for a person to squeeze in. The students eagerly formed lines in their groups, thrilled and ready to explore what lay ahead.

As they moved through the passage, they were greeted by a series of fascinating inscriptions carved into the walls. The ancient carvings, dimly lit by their flashlights, added a sense of magic and mystery to their adventure. Each inscription was carefully made, and the students took their time, fascinated by the stories and details these carvings revealed. The cave seemed to come alive with history, and the students felt a mix of wonder and curiosity as they examined the inscriptions, each one adding a new layer to their sense of discovery.

As the students continued deeper into the cave, the atmosphere became even more intriguing. The air grew cooler and the echoes of their footsteps softly bounced off the cavern walls.

The flickering lights from the torches revealed more intricate details in the carvings—some depicted ancient symbols, while others showed scenes of daily life from long ago. The cave's natural formations, like stalactites and stalagmites, added to the sense of wonder, making the environment feel both ancient and alive. Every new corner they turned seemed to uncover something new, fueling their excitement and imagination. The students felt like they were stepping back in time, uncovering secrets that had been hidden for centuries.

Mira, Elena and Xavier found one inscription and they started to read the inscriptions.

In the forest's dark embrace, shadows fall,
Ancient trees whisper warnings to all.
Beneath the canopy where dangers creep,
Hidden creatures in silence sleep.

Eyes that gleam and growls that fright,
Prowling beasts come alive at night
From the snarl of a lurking foe,
To the rustling where dangers grow.

Heed this warning as you tread,
For peril walks where light has fled.
In this forest, dark and wild,
Danger awaits with a hidden smile.

Once they read the inscription they felt something dangerous was awaiting them. As Elena Silently noted down the poem, Mira called out the guide, Sir, can you please explain what this means. It sounds like there is some danger. Should we be really going inside? "Do not worry, children," The guide said with a reassuring smile, "We have thoroughly examined this area, and there is no real danger here. The stories and warnings you might have heard are remnants of the past. It's likely that the people who once inhabited this place created these tales to protect the site from unwanted visitors. Historically, this area might have been used as a refuge during times of war or conflict. The warnings and mysterious accounts served as a deterrent to ensure that only those who truly respected or needed the sanctuary would find their way here. Today, we can explore this fascinating site safely, confident that we are well-prepared and guided by our careful exploration."

Feeling reassured, the trio continued along the path. As they ventured deeper into the cave, they marveled at the drawings etched into the walls. The artwork depicted a variety of wild animals: fierce lions, powerful tigers, and sinuous serpents, all of which they had seen before. However, there were also strange and unfamiliar creatures among the drawings—animals they had never encountered.

Xavier paused in front of a particularly intriguing drawing, causing Mira and Elena to call out to him, urging him to catch up. When he didn't move, the two girls hurried back to see what had captured his attention. There, on the cave wall, was a painting they had missed earlier. The image depicted an elderly man handing something to a young girl, while a procession of animals—lions, tigers, and serpents—followed her as she walked away. The trio felt an eerie chill as they studied the drawing, sensing that the scene seemed strikingly real. The detail and emotion in the artwork gave them the unsettling feeling that it was more than just a depiction; it was as if the events had been captured in time, conveying a story or legend from the cave's ancient past that was still very much alive in its portrayal. By now the trio started to fall behind the rest of the students. They wanted to see each and everything very carefully. They don't want to miss anything.

There were many other carvings of the young girl. The drawings seemed to show the girl performing acts of magic, with some scenes illustrating her surrounded by a glowing aura or casting spells that made the animals obey her commands. The way the animals were depicted—both in awe and in action—suggested a deep connection between the girl and the creatures. The intricate details of the carvings made it appear as if the girl possessed mystical powers.

The trio didn't realize that they were not on the path anymore. They continued walking looking at the wall, leading them to miss the path. They continued deeper away from the path!!.

Then there was another inscription.

In the forest where shadows play,
A creeping vine winds along the way.
Its touch is gentle, soft, and sly,
Yet it holds a secret to mystify.

If you brush against its leafy thread,
The path you've known will soon be shed.
The route you followed, clear and bright,
Will vanish, lost from the sight.

But listen well, for a passage hides,
Where ancient walls and darkness bide.
A hidden door, though hard to find,
Will lead you through, if you're aligned.

Once you enter, the only way out,
Is to solve the mystery without a doubt.
No way out until you see,
The clues that set the passage free.

So heed this clue as you explore,
Beware the vine on the forest floor.
For once you touch its winding line,
The way ahead will not be kind.

And if you wander, feeling lost,
Fear not the dark or the frost.
For with a heart that's pure and bold,
A guardian angel will unfold.

Elena noted down this as well. Mira wondered loudly, "I wonder why they keep talking about the forest. Do they mean the forest outside?". "Not sure", said Xavier. Suddenly they realized they were not on the path.

They panicked and leaned over the wall. BOOM!!. The wall turned and pulled the trio inside.

CHAPTER SIX

THE GLOWING CRYSTAL

As the wall suddenly pulled them inside, the trio violently jolted off balance. The intense force pressed against them, compressing their bodies and making it hard to breathe. The unexpected movement disoriented them, leaving them struggling to stay upright as the world spun around them. Colliding with the floor or nearby surfaces, their muscles tensed in an instinctive attempt to brace against the chaos.

Gasping and disoriented, they scrambled to their feet, their minds racing to comprehend what had just happened.

"What just happened?!" Xavier exclaimed, his voice filled with panic. "We were in that cave and now we're... here! What is this place? We shouldn't be here. We need to go back!"

The trio started shouting for help and banging on the wall, but their cries echoed unanswered. The wall remained solid and unyielding, and despite their desperate efforts to find a way back, nothing changed. On the other side, no one realized they were missing.

Desperation took hold as they pushed against the wall and tried various methods to return, but each attempt proved fruitless. The reality of their predicament began to sink in. Mira and Elena, unable to sit still, started to pace back and forth in the dimly lit cave. The meager light allowed them to see each other's faces, but details remained obscured in the gloom.

Xavier took a deep breath, remembering his mother's advice about staying calm in crisis situations. Her words echoed in his mind: "Stay calm and think clearly."

He gathered his thoughts and spoke to Mira and Elena, his voice steady despite the tension. "My mom always told me to stay calm and think things through when we're in a tough spot. Let's focus on what we can do to improve our situation."

Mira said "I wish we were allowed to carry a smartphone, at least we could call someone."

Suddenly, Xavier called out, "My mom gifted me a smart watch. I can call her in case of an emergency!. She can also track me to this place.!!"

Both Mira and Elena dashed towards Xavier, their hearts racing with renewed hope. But their excitement quickly turned to disappointment when they discovered there was no signal. Defeated, they slumped to the ground, their earlier energy drained. They sat together, trying to think through their next steps, grappling with the weight of their situation and searching for a new plan.

They began to examine their surroundings more closely. The space they had been forced into resembling a closed room with no visible doors. The walls were smooth and unyielding, and there were no apparent exits or openings.

Elena, trying to maintain a semblance of calm, suggested, "Let's just wait here. I'm sure someone will come for us soon. Our parents will realize we're missing, and they'll come looking." If they bring down the wall where we were last seen, I'm sure they will find us."

Despite their initial hope, every time they thought they heard a sound, their cries for help went unanswered. As time wore on, hunger began to gnaw at them. They sifted through their lunch boxes, sharing the scant provisions they had and making the decision to save some for later.

As they continued to wait, they noticed the cave growing darker. The faint light from the crack in the wall, which had previously offered some illumination, seemed to be fading. They realized that it must be getting dark outside.

"I'm feeling really tired," Elena said, rubbing her eyes. "Maybe we should get some sleep."

"But what if someone comes looking for us?" Xavier protested. "We need to stay alert."

Mira, trying to be practical, suggested, "How about we take shifts? One person can stay awake while the others sleep. When one of us gets too tired, the next person can take over. How does that sound?"

The idea seemed reasonable under the circumstances, and the others agreed.

"I'm not feeling sleepy right now," Mira said. "Let me take the first shift."

With Mira settling into a makeshift watch, Elena and Xavier lay down on the cold floor, doing their best to find some comfort. The uneasy silence was occasionally broken by Mira's attempts to stay alert, her eyes scanning the dark surroundings for any sign of rescue or change. The trio hoped that this plan would help them endure until someone noticed they were missing and came to their aid.

As Mira stood on watch, a strange sensation tugged at her senses. It felt as though someone was calling her name, faint and distant, like a whisper carried by the wind. She blinked and strained her ears, but the sound quickly faded, leaving her questioning whether it was real or just a figment of her imagination.

Determined to stay focused, she shook off the unsettling feeling and reminded herself of their predicament. "If we get out of here," she thought, "I want to be more like Elena. Calm, collected, and able to keep everyone together."

With renewed resolve, Mira continued her watch, her thoughts drifting between the hope of rescue and her desire to emulate Elena's steady leadership. The silence of the dark, unfamiliar space wrapped around her, but she held onto the belief that they would find their way back home.

Once she started to feel tired, she woke Xavier up and tried to get some sleep. Xavier, who was in the middle of the sleep, couldn't stay up longer. He dozed off, otherwise maybe he would have noticed a pair of glowing eyes, watching them.

Mira's sleep was troubled from the moment she closed her eyes. Her dreams twisted into a series of nightmarish visions, each more unsettling than the last. In one particularly vivid nightmare, she found herself being chased by a creature from the carvings on the wall.

The monster was towering and menacing, standing around 8 feet tall. It was impossibly thin, with a skinny, skeletal frame that seemed to stretch unnaturally. Its face was a horrifying sight: a single, eerie eye set in the center of its forehead, and a long, writhing tongue that flicked out menacingly. The creature's two hands were unnervingly positioned on its back, and its feet, devoid of toes, seemed to glide across the ground with unsettling smoothness.

The creature moved with a nightmarish grace, and Mira could feel the terror of being pursued by it, her heart racing as she struggled to escape. The nightmare seemed endless, the creature always just a step behind, its gaze fixed and unrelenting.

She awoke with a startle, drenched in sweat and breathing heavily. The images from her dream clung to her mind, leaving her with a deep sense of dread. Mira took a few moments to collect herself, trying to shake off the remnants of fear and the bizarre vision. Despite the terror of her nightmare, she knew she had to remain vigilant and strong for her friends.

Mira rubbed her eyes and looked around. She noticed Elena sitting calmly with a book in her hands, absorbed in her reading under a sliver ray of sunlight that had managed to pierce the darkness through a crack in the cave wall.

"Seriously, Elena?" Mira exclaimed, her voice tinged with disbelief. "We're stuck here, and you're studying for your exam?!"

Elena looked up, her concentration momentarily broken. "I'm not studying for my exam, Mira!" she said with a touch of frustration. "I'm trying to find clues to get us out of here. Remember the puzzles we saw outside? I'm trying to understand them."

Mira's eyes widened as she realized Elena's true intent. "Did you actually take notes?" she asked, her voice filled with relief and admiration. "I love you so much!"

Seeing Mira's enthusiasm, Elena nodded. "Yes, I did. Let's work on it together."

The two sisters huddled around the book and any notes Elena had made, focusing on deciphering the puzzle. Do you see both these poems talk about some forest, But I don't see any forest here. But read this part

> *Once you enter, the only way out,*
> *Is to solve the mystery without a doubt.*
> *No way out until you see,*
> *The clues that set the passage free.*

There must be some clues here, if we managed to solve this, it might take us out. Let's find the clue, by then Xavier also woke up from his sleep and they decided to find clues.

"But what can we do with this little light? We cannot see much," Elena said, her frustration evident. "First, we need to think about how to get more light."

Mira quickly responded, "Do we have a torch, a lighter, or a matchbox? We could start a small fire to help us see better." She continued, "If we find some stones, we could rub them together to create a spark."

"Good idea," Elena said, nodding. "Let's gather some flammable materials first and find two stones that might work for striking a spark."

The trio set to work, scouring the cave for anything that could be used to start a fire. They gathered scraps of paper from their lunch boxes, dried leaves, and other potentially flammable materials. Meanwhile, they also searched for two suitable stones that might generate a spark when struck together.

As Xavier crawled around looking for stones and leaves, his watch caught a beam of the small sunlight that was filtering through the crack. The reflection caught his eye, and he shouted with excitement, "Look! My watch is reflecting the light. Maybe we can use this!"

Elena and Mira rushed over to see what Xavier was pointing at. The watch's reflective surface created a tiny, focused beam of light. They realized it could serve as a tool to illuminate the dark corners of the cave.

With renewed hope, they carefully positioned the watch to direct the beam of light onto the walls and floor. "This is incredible," Elena said, adjusting the angle of the watch. "The light is helping us see things we couldn't before."

However, as they continued to search, a sense of frustration began to set in. The cave was vast, and it quickly became apparent that examining every inch would be a daunting, time-consuming task.

"This might take forever," Mira said, her voice tinged with worry. "We don't have all the time in the world."

Despite their growing disappointment, they realized they had no better option. The beam of light from the watch was their best tool for now, and they had to make the most of it.

After a period of painstaking examination, the beam of light from the watch finally fell on a spot that caught their attention. There, embedded in the wall, was a crystal-like object. As the light hit the crystal, something extraordinary happened—the entire room suddenly illuminated with a brilliant glow.

The trio gasped in amazement as the crystal seemed to absorb and amplify the light, casting a warm, bright radiance throughout the cave. The once dimly lit space was now vividly illuminated, revealing every corner and detail.

"This is incredible!" Elena exclaimed, her eyes wide with astonishment. "The crystal must be reflecting and dispersing the light. It's lighting up the whole room!"

The newfound brightness allowed them to see clearly, and they noticed details in the cave's markings that had previously been hidden in the darkness. With the room now fully illuminated, they could explore more effectively and potentially uncover more clues about their escape.

"This changes everything," Mira said, her voice filled with hope. "Let's take a closer look at the entire cave now that we can see everything."

They began to examine the cave with renewed energy, their spirits lifted by the sudden transformation of their surroundings. The glowing crystal had turned their desperate situation into one filled with possibility, offering a beacon of hope in their quest for freedom.

CHAPTER SEVEN

RIDDLES OF THE ANCIENT CAVE

Once fully lit, the cave revealed numerous symbols and inscriptions on the walls. They set the watch on the floor pointing to the crystal and began examining the clues, but the sheer volume of markings and artifacts was overwhelming. "There are so many things—where do we start?" they wondered, trying to make sense of the intricate details and decide on their next move.

They started to go through symbols and riddles. Then Mira spotted one riddle, it was there on the wall through which they had come to this room.

> *To start your quest and find your way,*
> *Here's the first clue to guide your play.*
> *Search where secret and shadows blend,*
> *And there is the next clue you'll need".*

Elena and Xavier gathered around Mira, peering at the newly discovered clue. Elena read the clue aloud and said, "This is indeed a clue, it says it's the first riddle, and it's pointing to the next clue. That means there is a series of clues we need to solve.

If we get one wrong, we will never get out!" Her tone was serious, reflecting the gravity of their situation.

Xavier, trying to stay positive, chimed in, "Don't worry, Elena. We'll get through this. Remember the escape room we visited during our last school trip? We managed to escape in record time—no one's beaten that record even to this day."

Mira, glancing around the dimly lit cave, added, "Let's hope so. We're running low on food and water. We need to think fast and find a way out of here as soon as possible."

The trio huddled together, the urgency of their situation heightening their focus. They knew that solving each riddle was crucial for their escape and that their survival depended on their quick thinking and teamwork.

Elena, Xavier, and Mira stood in the room, their eyes scanning the walls for any sign of the hidden clue. The phrase "Search where secrets and shadows blend" echoed in their minds. "It's definitely pointing to some place in the room," Mira mused. "But what does it mean by 'secret and shadows'?" She continued, her brow furrowing in concentration.

"There are many symbols here," Elena said, pointing to the wall covered with various marks. "Are we supposed to see them in the shadows? But which secret in particular are we looking for?"

Xavier, growing frustrated with the complexity of the clue, exclaimed, "This room itself is a secret, which is pointing to another secret!"

"That's it!" Mira suddenly exclaimed. "The secret is the room itself. Now let's find a place covered by shadows."

The trio quickly turned their attention to the shadows cast by the objects and features in the room. They identified three distinct shadows and began their search. Each of them examined a different shadow carefully, running their hands along the edges and peering closely into the darkened areas.

After some time of thorough investigation, Mira noticed something unusual. She pressed on a specific spot in one of the shadows, and with a soft click, a small drawer slid out from the wall. The unexpected sound of the mechanism was followed by a gasp of surprise from Mira.

Elena, watching Mira's success, decided to try the same approach. She pressed on another spot in her shadow and, to her delight, found a hidden compartment springing open as well.

From the drawer, Mira carefully retrieved a small, terracotta-colored bird-shaped object. The object had a distinctive appearance with a long, curved neck and a rounded body. Intricate details adorned its surface: there were carefully drawn eyes, wings, and other embellishments that gave it a lifelike quality. On the top of its head was a small hole, and the curved neck extended into a mouthpiece, suggesting that it might be some sort of ancient or ceremonial artifact, possibly used for producing sound. The object's design hinted at both artistic craftsmanship and functional purpose, with the mouthpiece indicating it could be used to blow air through, possibly creating a sound or signal. Mira placed it on her lips and gently blew into the mouthpiece. But nothing happened.

While Mira was busy with the bird-shaped artifact, Elena was examining the second drawer she had discovered. She carefully pulled out the drawer and found a small, ornate mirror nestled inside.

Elena picked up the mirror and examined it closely. The glass was clear, though slightly fogged from age. The frame was adorned with symbols and designs that matched some of the markings on the walls of the room.

Curious, Elena tilted the mirror at various angles, trying to see if it revealed anything hidden. As she adjusted its position, she realized that the mirror was reflecting parts of the room that weren't visible from where she stood through naked eyes. It seemed to focus light and shadows in a way that highlighted hidden markings or features on the walls that had previously gone unnoticed.

Excited by this discovery, Elena called out to Mira and Xavier. "Look at this! The mirror seems to show things we can't see directly. Maybe it's part of solving the next clue. We should use it to examine the room more closely."

Mira and Xavier joined Elena in exploring the mirrored reflections, carefully analyzing the new details that became visible. The mirror's unique properties offered a new perspective on the room.

When they moved the mirror and pointed it to the crystal, a beam of light fell on the mirror and its reflection fell on the wall. And on the reflection there was their second clue.

> *Guide me where the sun's rays fall,*
> *And light the room to heed the call.*
> *Seek the fragments strewn around,*
> *Combine them, and your path will unfold.*

In their excitement, the trio eagerly tackled the riddle: "Guide me where the sun's rays fall." They reasoned that the solution might involve pointing the mirror directly at the sun. They positioned the mirror in the sunlight, hoping for a revelation, but nothing changed.

"Perhaps we should remove the light from the crystal and examine it in complete darkness," Mira proposed. Despite their efforts, this approach also yielded no results.

They then tried using the mirror to reflect light onto the crystal, attempting to illuminate the entire room, but this, too, proved ineffective.

Finally, Elena offered a bold suggestion: "Could it be asking us to set the room on fire?"

Upon hearing Elena's suggestion, the others exchanged concerned glances. Mira shook her head, her expression a mix of disbelief and apprehension. "Setting the room on fire? That's a bit extreme and dangerous," she said.

Xavier, always the cautious one, added, "I don't think it's practical or safe. There's got to be another way to solve this riddle."

Elena's idea seemed a bit extreme, They all agreed that, while the suggestion was creative, it wasn't worth the risk. They decided to revisit their previous attempts, looking for any overlooked details or clues that might lead them to a safer solution.

Even after working for an hour they couldn't come up with any solution. Then Mira and Xavier agreed to Elena's suggestion. But they decided to be extra cautious. They pointed the sun rays to the earlier collected flammable materials. After some time the fire ignited, and quickly it got spread, burning nothing but a thin layer of dried grass revealing hidden things underneath. They were watchful enough not letting fire go out of control.

They relit the room with the help of the crystal and began searching for fragments scattered across the ground. The room revealed several intriguing items, but despite their efforts to piece them together, the trio couldn't make any progress. Exhausted from their attempts, they decided to take a break.

As the others rested, Mira's curiosity led her to a collection of bones on the floor. She began to examine them closely, wondering what kind of animal they might belong to. Intrigued, she started arranging the bones, her mind racing with possibilities.

After some time, Mira successfully arranged the bones into a complete skeleton. She called over the others to show her discovery. "Look, it's a skeleton of a deer," she said, her curiosity piqued.

Xavier, examining the skeleton closely, noticed something that Mira had missed. "Actually, look at those horns over there, maybe it's not a doe—they're from a stag," he pointed out. With careful precision, he joined the horns to the deer's head, completing the image of a stag.

The trio stood back, admiring their work on the assembled stag's skeleton. They suddenly noticed a strange, shimmering light emanating from the assembled skeleton. Without warning, the bones began to shift and move, seemingly on their own. The skeleton, once lifeless, now seemed to pulse with a faint, ethereal glow.

The bones reassembled themselves with a series of clicking sounds, the once-disjointed parts coming together with uncanny precision. The rib cage expanded and contracted as if taking breaths, and the skull's empty eye sockets glowed with a soft, otherworldly light. The stag's legs, previously rigid and still, flexed and moved with a natural grace.

In a breathtaking transformation, the skeleton's form became more defined, muscles seemingly appearing out of thin air. The once bare bones were now covered with a translucent, shining membrane that gave the illusion of flesh and fur. The stag's antlers, intricate and majestic, seemed to grow and take on a vibrant, almost living quality.

With a powerful, graceful motion, the newly animated stag lifted its head and let out a low, resonant call, echoing through the cave. It then bounded forward with surprising agility, its hooves making soft, echoing sounds against the cave floor. The creature moved with purpose, then it looked at the shocked friends, blinked its eyes and then bolted towards the wall.

"Let's go!!" cried Elena, In a flurry of panic and excitement, the trio quickly gathered their belongings and chased after the stag. The wall opened a doorway and they ran through it feeling relieved.

Once they reached the other side, the door vanished behind them, leaving no trace of its existence. The trio was left standing in a new, unfamiliar area, with no visible sign of the way they had just come from.

CHAPTER EIGHT

THE WISHING WELL

By the time they were out of the door, the stag had vanished. They wondered where it could have gone. Despite this, they felt a sense of pride in their accomplishment, grateful for their quick thinking and ability to stay composed under pressure.

"Did you see that?!" exclaimed Mira. "The door has vanished! If we had waited just another minute, we would have been stuck there forever!"

Elena took a deep breath and said, "Well, we made it out in time. Let's stay focused and figure out where we are now."

"Is this the same place where we started?" Xavier asked, squinting at the new surroundings.

"I don't think so," Elena replied, shaking her head. "The cave we were in before was gray, but look at this—everything here is white. It's definitely different."

Mira glanced around, noting the contrast in colors and the distinct atmosphere of the new room. "It does feel different. The glow is new too. Let's explore and see if we can find any clues to confirm where we are."

"Let's continue in this passage," Elena said firmly. "The only way out is to go forward—we don't have any other option."

The trio nodded in agreement and began to move forward cautiously. By now, they understood the gravity of their situation: they were deep into the game, and their decisions could have significant consequences. Every misstep could lead them into even greater trouble, so they needed to stay vigilant and thoughtful as they progressed.

"Guys, do you remember all that poem about a forest, maybe the deer is going there. We should try to find it. It should have gone this way, unless there is another secret door." said Mira.

So they decided to move faster in the passage, determined to catch up with the deer. At one point of time, the passage was divided into 3 tunnels.

"Where should we go now?" Xavier asked, scanning the passageway.

"Let's look for any clues," Elena suggested. They began examining their surroundings, but no clues were immediately visible.

Xavier then proposed, "Why don't we each take a separate tunnel and try to find something?"

"Absolutely not!" Elena responded firmly. "We shouldn't separate, no matter what. What if there's some unexpected danger ahead? We won't be able to handle it alone. After all, we're just kids."

Her reasoning made sense to the group. They agreed to stick together, knowing that their best chance of success and safety was to face whatever lay ahead as a team.

"Let's all go into the same tunnel," Mira suggested. "We'll venture a certain distance into one tunnel and look for any clues. If we don't find anything, we can return and try the next tunnel."

The others nodded in agreement. With a unified decision, they carefully entered the first tunnel, determined to thoroughly search it before moving on to explore the other passages. They walked inside that tunnel for over five minutes but did not find any clues. So, they decided to head back and entered the second tunnel. They walked around for a minute or so when Mira pointed at some droppings on the ground.

"Look at this," Mira said, pointing at some droppings on the ground. "These look like deer droppings. It must have gone this way!" So They decided to continue exploring the second tunnel.

They continued walking for a long time. Elena, who was leading the way, nearly stumbled. "Watch out!" Xavier shouted as he quickly pulled her back. The trio stood in front of a massive well. They began to carefully examine the well.

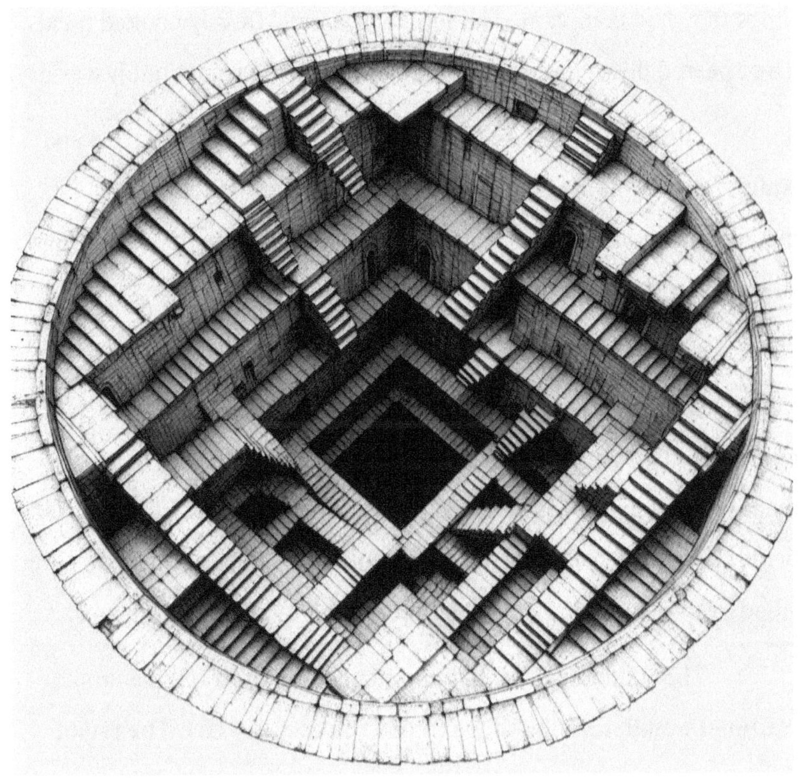

The well was extremely wide, reaching about 100 feet deep. They began to carefully examine it, noting the steps that spiraled down in various directions, forming a complex pattern. Between these patterns, they spotted a closed window-like structure, intriguing and mysterious.

The trio was extremely hungry and thirsty by now. They had nothing to eat and no water to drink. They began to regret all the times they had complained about their parents' freshly cooked meals. They peered down the well, hoping to find some water, but it was dry.

Disappointed, Elena said, "I wish there was some food and water. I can't continue anymore." Her voice was tinged with exhaustion and frustration as the trio stared at the empty well, their stomachs rumbling in unison.

Suddenly, there was a thunderous BOOM! The ground trembled slightly, and a dazzling flash of light illuminated the dark tunnel. To their amazement, a grand feast materialized in front of them. The table was laden with an assortment of food: freshly baked bread, juicy fruits, cheese, and many more. A large jug of clear water stood prominently in the center, surrounded by gleaming glasses.

The food looked both tempting and comforting, the aroma wafting through the air and making their mouths water. The jug of water seemed to promise relief from their intense thirst. The appearance of this unexpected bounty was almost magical, a stark contrast to their earlier despair.

At that moment, the trio didn't think about the possible consequences of eating such food. Their hunger and thirst were overwhelming, and the sight of the feast made them forget their previous caution. They quickly gathered around the table, eagerly reaching for the food and water, their earlier worries momentarily forgotten in the face of such an incredible and timely provision.

Once they had filled their tummies with the delicious food and water, a sense of satisfaction washed over them. Their earlier exhaustion and thirst were now forgotten. However, as they began to relax, a new concern arose.

"Wait a minute," Mira said, her brow furrowing. "How did the food and water just appear here? Was this some kind of test?"

Xavier's face paled slightly as he considered the possibility. "Maybe we weren't supposed to eat it. What if this was a trap or a test of some sort?"

Elena nodded, her earlier relief giving way to worry. "You're right. We were so hungry and thirsty that we didn't think about the consequences. What if this was a trick to see if we'd make a mistake?"

The trio looked at each other, their previous delight replaced by a growing unease. They had been so focused on satisfying their immediate needs that they hadn't considered the potential risks of consuming the unexpected feast.

The trio, now more cautious but still determined, decided to fill their bags with fruits and water, ensuring they had enough supplies for the journey ahead. As they did that, Xavier voiced a lingering concern, "I wish we knew where we are."

Suddenly, a voice echoed through the well, deep and resonant. "You are inside a wishing well," it intoned. "Give me your wish, and I shall fulfill it. "

The voice seemed to emanate from the very walls of the well, reverberating around them. The trio exchanged surprised glances, the revelation that they were in a wishing well adding an unexpected twist to their adventure.

Elena, still processing the strange turn of events, asked hesitantly, "If you can fulfill our wish, can you help us go back to our home?"

The voice responded with a hint of amusement, "I can grant wishes, but my powers are limited. I can provide you with information or assistance, but I cannot return you to where you started. Your path forward is still up to you."

Mira, overwhelmed by a sudden surge of emotion, blurted out, "I wish to see my parents."

In an instant, the air glowed with a soft, ethereal light. The trio watched in awe as two separate projections materialized before them. One projected Mira's mother and the other projected her father. They both were working in their respective offices as if nothing had happened.

Mira's eyes welled up with tears as she saw her parents, her heart aching. "How is this possible?" she asked, her voice trembling.

"Didn't they realize we're missing? They're still in their office, like nothing has happened. Should we really go back, why can't we just stay here, the well can give us food and anything we need."

Elena and Xavier looked on with concern. They too were struck by the eerie calm of the projections.

Elena put a comforting hand on Mira's shoulder. "Maybe it's not that they don't care or haven't noticed. It could be that this world works differently from ours. Maybe it's not their current state but more like a recording from the past. None of this might be real, and we could be stuck here forever if we don't keep moving. There might be dangers we haven't encountered yet. We need to stay focused and keep going. But we can rest here for the night."

Mira nodded slowly, her tears drying as she processed Elena's words. The reality of their situation settled in again. The projections of her parents, while deeply distressing, were a reminder of the urgency of their quest. They had to navigate through this world and find a way back, no matter the challenges they faced.

Exhausted from another long day of exploration and anxiety, the trio realized the importance of rest. Elena voiced their collective need, saying, "I wish we could find a comfortable place to get some sleep!"

As soon as her words left her lips, the air around them shimmered and a soothing, warm light enveloped their surroundings.

The labyrinth seemed to shift and transform, and before their eyes, a cozy, inviting resting area appeared.

The new space resembled a quaint, serene retreat. Soft, plush bedding was neatly arranged on a raised platform, surrounded by cushioned seating and warm, flickering lanterns that cast a gentle, calming glow. The walls were adorned with soothing colors, and a subtle, fragrant breeze carried a hint of lavender and cedar.

They stood in awe for a moment, appreciating the unexpected comfort that had manifested. The transformation was so sudden and serene that it felt almost dreamlike.

"This is incredible," Mira said, her eyes wide with relief. "It's like a perfect haven after everything we've been through."

Elena and Xavier agreed, their fatigue melting away at the sight of their new resting place. They quickly made themselves comfortable, sinking into the soft bedding and letting the tension of their journey dissipate.

As they settled in, the trio felt a profound sense of gratitude and peace. They knew that tomorrow would bring new challenges, but for now, they could rest and recharge in the comfort of their unexpected sanctuary.

CHAPTER NINE

RESCUE IN THE WILDERNESS

As morning arrived, the trio woke up feeling refreshed and ready to tackle the challenges ahead. They packed up their bags with the remaining fruits and water, preparing for the day's journey with renewed determination.

"Let's keep moving forward," Elena said, her voice filled with resolve. "We have to find a way out of this tunnel and figure out what's really going on."

Xavier and Mira nodded in agreement. Despite their previous doubts and exhaustion, they were motivated by their sense of purpose and the goal of escaping the mysterious situation they had found themselves in.

Suddenly, a shared realization dawned upon them, and in unison, they said, "We wish to move forward."

As soon as the words left their lips, the cozy resting area began to fade away. The warm light that had enveloped them gradually dimmed, and the comforting surroundings transformed back into the labyrinth's intricate passages. The walls, once soft and inviting, now took on their familiar, enigmatic appearance.

Before them, a new path emerged, distinct from the previous tunnels. It was illuminated by a soft, guiding light that seemed to beckon them forward.

"Looks like we're back on track," Xavier said, his voice carrying a mix of relief and determination. "Let's see where this new path leads us."

As they emerged from the window-like opening, a vast forest unfolded before them, bathed in the soft light of dawn. The trees stood tall and majestic, their trunks cloaked in moss and their leaves whispering secrets in the gentle breeze. The forest floor was a vibrant mosaic of rich green ferns, colorful wildflowers, and patches of sunlight that filtered through the dense canopy above.

A narrow trail wound through the undergrowth, barely visible yet inviting exploration. The path was flanked by clusters of vibrant mushrooms and twisting vines, suggesting a world alive with magic and mystery.

The air was filled with the fresh, earthy scent of moss and pine, mingling with the sweet aroma of blooming flowers. Birds chirped melodiously, and the distant sound of a babbling brook added a serene soundtrack to the scene. The forest seemed to stretch endlessly, with ancient trees forming natural archways and pathways.

The trio stood in awe. This new environment felt both enchanting and mysterious, offering a complete contrast to the dark, confining tunnels they had traversed previously. The forest's beauty and tranquility were captivating, but they also sensed that this place held its own set of challenges and secrets.

"Wow, look at this place," Mira said, her eyes wide with wonder. "It's incredible."

"Yes," Elena agreed, "but we can't let our guard down. We don't know what might be lurking here."

Xavier nodded, his gaze scanning the forest for any signs of danger or clues. "Let's stay alert and see if we can find any leads. We should stick together and follow the trail cautiously ."

As they stepped onto the trail, the forest seemed to come alive around them. Each step crunched softly on the carpet of leaves, and the sunlight danced across their faces, highlighting the intricate details of the forest's beauty.

But as they ventured deeper, the trail behind them began to fade, closing off their way back. They were fully committed to their adventure now, with no turning back. Each step forward felt like an invitation to discover the mysteries that lay ahead, urging them onward into the heart of the enchanted forest.

For the first three hours, the path was an easy slope, winding gently through the woods. The forest was predominantly pine, with towering trees that created a rich, green canopy overhead. Here and there, occasional maple trees added a splash of vibrant green, their new leaves catching the light and creating a lively contrast against the darker pines.

After three hours of steady walking, the terrain began to change. The path led them to a dramatic landscape where two mountains met, forming a rugged joint. Nestled between these towering peaks was a small, sparkling stream, its clear waters gently flowing over smooth stones. The stream flowed through the space, its tranquil flow a serene addition to the rugged beauty of the landscape.

The trio paused at the stream, taking in the stunning view of the mountains and the peaceful sound of the water.

Elena stopped and turned to her companions. "Let's take a break here and refill our bottles with this water. The path ahead climbs steeply up the mountain, and it's going to get a lot more challenging from here. This spot looks a bit safer, so we might as well relax and even take a short nap if we can."

Mira and Xavier agreed with a nod. They set down their bags and settled onto the ground, taking a moment to rest and enjoy the tranquility of the spot.

Xavier spotted a large rock and decided it would be a comfortable spot to rest. As he lowered himself onto the rock, he was suddenly jolted by an unexpected movement. The rock began to shift and slowly rise, causing Xavier to leap up in shock.

To his astonishment, the "rock" was actually a massive tortoise. Its shell, rugged and textured like the surrounding stones, had blended seamlessly with the natural environment. The tortoise's enormous, weathered shell was adorned with moss and small patches of lichen, making it nearly indistinguishable from the rocky terrain.

The tortoise's eyes blinked slowly and calmly, seemingly unfazed by Xavier's reaction. It moved with deliberate, measured motions, its heavy limbs creating a gentle, rhythmic sound against the ground. The realization that he had been sitting on such a remarkable creature left Xavier both awestruck and a bit embarrassed.

Mira and Elena, having witnessed the commotion, approached with curiosity. "What happened?" Mira asked, peering at the giant tortoise.

Xavier, still catching his breath, pointed at the tortoise with a mix of relief and fascination. "I thought this rock was just a place to sit, but it's actually a giant tortoise!"

Elena and Mira exchanged amused glances, their initial concern giving way to laughter.

As they relaxed by the stream, their peaceful moment was abruptly shattered by a distress call echoing through the forest. The trio froze, their heads snapping in the direction of the sound. Without thinking, they abandoned their plan to stay on the path and ran toward the source of the distress call.

Bursting through the underbrush, they stumbled upon a heartbreaking scene. A small squirrel was caught in the clutches of a snake, its tiny body swollen and struggling against the serpent's coils. The snake, a large and menacing creature with shimmering scales, had trapped the squirrel and was tightening its grip.

The trio's hearts raced with panic as they took in the sight. Mira's eyes widened in horror, and she gasped, "We have to do something! We can't just leave it like this!"

Elena and Xavier, equally distressed, exchanged desperate glances. They knew they had to act quickly, but they weren't sure what to do. Instinctively, they began shouting and waving their arms in an attempt to scare the snake away.

"Hey! Get away from it!" Elena shouted, her voice trembling with urgency. She grabbed a nearby stick and began waving it furiously at the snake, hoping to draw its attention.

Xavier joined in, his voice rising in a frantic pitch. "Shoo! Go away! Leave it alone!"

Mira, although scared, picked up a few small stones and started throwing them in the direction of the snake, trying to hit it without harming the squirrel.

The commotion they created seemed to have some effect. The snake paused its constriction, its head flicking back and forth as it assessed the new threat. The squirrel's cries became more frantic, but it continued to struggle, its tiny paws flailing helplessly.

"Come on, snake, go away!" Xavier urged, his voice strained. The snake, now visibly agitated, began to loosen its grip and slowly retreated, slithering away into the underbrush with a menacing rustle.

As the snake disappeared, the trio rushed to the squirrel's side. The poor creature was gasping for breath, its little body trembling with fear. Mira carefully examined the squirrel, her hands trembling as she tried to assess the damage.

"It looks like it's badly hurt," Mira said softly, her voice filled with concern. "We need to help him".

Elena nodded, her face pale with worry. "Let's take it back near our bags, I have some first aid supplies, but I'm not sure if they'll help the squirrel."

The trio gently picked up the injured squirrel, being careful not to cause any further harm. They carefully carried it back to their spot, by their bags. They laid it gently on a soft patch of grass near their bags. Elena quickly took charge, preparing to administer first aid. She cleaned the squirrel's wounds with water and applied a makeshift bandage to the most serious injuries.

"We did what we could," Xavier said, trying to steady his shaking hands. "Let's keep an eye on it and see if there's anything more we can do."

"Let's stay here until tomorrow morning," Mira suggested thoughtfully. "The squirrel should feel better by then. We can make sure it's strong enough to return to the wild and then continue our journey in the morning."

The trio didn't have the heart to leave the squirrel, so they all decided to pause the journey until tomorrow.

Xavier said thinking, "This forest looks really dangerous, how do we ensure our safety through the night?" Then suddenly Elena remembered the mirror she found in the hidden room, and she used it to reveal a concealed place to rest for the night.

As night fell, they gathered around the fire they had built to keep themselves warm and safe. The flickering flames cast shadows on their faces, reflecting the tension and concern they felt. They knew that their encounter with the snake had been a stark reminder of the dangers lurking in the forest and there are many more to come. As they sat by the stream, watching over the wounded squirrel, they couldn't help but feel a sense of unease about what other challenges ahead on their journey.

CHAPTER TEN

RIDDLES OF THE GUARDIAN

The next morning, Mira slowly woke to the forest's lively atmosphere, disoriented from her unexpected slumber. She had been keeping watch, but she must have fallen asleep without realizing it. As she stirred, her first thought was of the squirrel. She quickly turned to check on it, her heart pounding with concern.

To her surprise and relief, she saw the squirrel on its feet, although with a slight limp. It was moving around with cautious but determined steps, a hopeful sign of recovery. Mira watched with a mixture of amazement and satisfaction, grateful that their efforts to help the little creature had not been in vain.

Mira gently woke the others, and they were all relieved to see that the squirrel had begun to recover. Its slight limp was a hopeful sign that it was on the mend. With renewed spirits, they refreshed themselves, enjoyed a meal, and left some fruits for their little friend.

As Mira and her companions began their ascent up the hill, the rustling of leaves and the distant call of a squirrel reached their ears. The squirrel's voice, tinged with urgency, seemed to cut through the tranquil morning air.

"We're heading towards freedom," Mira shouted back, her voice firm but gentle. "You stay here and catch your breath. We need to find our way back home, but we hope you find your own path soon. Rest up and take care!".

Mira noticed the squirrel limping after them, clearly determined to join their journey despite its obvious discomfort. With a soft sigh, she crouched down and gently picked up the small creature.

"Alright, little guy," Mira said with a warm smile, cradling the squirrel in her hands. "If you're set on coming with us, I'll carry you."

The squirrel looked up at her with a mix of gratitude and stubbornness. Mira adjusted her hold to make sure the tiny animal was comfortable and secure.

With the squirrel now officially joining their journey and comfortably nestled in Mira's hands, the group continued their ascent up the hill. The sun climbed higher, casting a warm glow over their path. Mira's steady steps and Xavier's upbeat chatter helped lift everyone's spirits, while the squirrel seemed to settle in comfortably, his earlier distress replaced by a sense of security.

As they climbed, the landscape began to unfold before them, revealing sweeping views of the valley below and the distant outlines of the mountain ranges.

After hours of climbing, the group finally reached the summit. The sun, now dipping towards the west, cast a warm, golden light over the landscape. The horizon stretched out magnificently, revealing an expansive view of rolling hills, shimmering lakes, and distant mountains.

Elena, her breath slightly labored from the climb, pointed towards the breathtaking panorama. "Look at that view," she said, her voice filled with awe. "It's incredible."

The others gathered around, taking in the scene with a mix of exhaustion and wonder. The beauty of the landscape made their hard work feel worthwhile, and for a moment, the world seemed to stretch out endlessly before them.

Elena's gaze followed Mira's excited cry. Mira was standing near a large rock, where a small crowd of birds had gathered, chirping and flapping around the squirrel, who was perched on her shoulder.

"Look!" Mira said, her eyes wide with amazement. "This squirrel seems very famous in these woods. Many birds are coming closer to me, and they seem to be communicating with him!"

The birds fluttered around the Squirrel, their songs forming a melodious chorus. The Squirrel, seemingly unfazed, appeared to be chattering back at them in a series of tiny squeaks and tail flicks. The sight was both enchanting and surreal, as if he had a special connection with the woodland creatures.

"Do you think he is some kind of woodland ambassador?" Xavier jokes, marveling at the scene.

Mira smiled, feeling a deep sense of wonder. "Maybe he is. It's like he's brought us into a special part of this place. It feels like we're witnessing something truly magical."

As the sun continued its descent, painting the sky in hues of orange and pink, the group stood in awe, enjoying the unexpected and delightful turn of their adventure.

But Elena was looking at something else. "Guys, look!! Look at that statue," she exclaimed, her voice filled with excitement.

The group turned their attention to where Elena was pointing. In the distance, they saw a massive statue rising from the forest floor, partially hidden by the surrounding trees. The statue's grandeur was evident even from afar.

"Let's go and take a closer look," Elena suggested.

They continued walking along their trail, and to their surprise, the statue appeared right in their path.

The giant sculpture, seemingly an extension of the natural rock, gazing right at them. Its massive, muscular form merged seamlessly with the stone, giving the impression that it had emerged organically from the earth itself. The statue's face, with its deep-set eyes and serious expression, exuded a sense of ancient wisdom and power.

The body of the sculpture was intricately textured to mirror the rough surface of the surrounding rock. Carved into its form were detailed natural elements, including cascading waterfalls and winding trees, which added to its majestic presence. The entire figure stood as a solemn structure against the rugged landscape, its imposing stature commanding respect.

As the group approached, they felt a blend of reverence and wonder. The statue seemed to hold the secrets of the land within its stone-carved heart, inviting them to explore its mysteries and perhaps uncover the ancient tales it might tell.

Behind the statue was a wide, pink river, its waters shimmering with a soft, rosy hue. The unusual color of the river seemed to glow against the rugged backdrop of the forest, adding a surreal and enchanting quality to the scene. The pink river meandered through the landscape, reflecting the late afternoon sunlight and casting a gentle, warm light over the surrounding area. Its presence added a mysterious allure to the already captivating setting, drawing the children's attention and curiosity.

"How do we cross this river", asked Mira nervously.

As the children approached the statue, its immense, weathered face seemed to come alive. A soft, rumbling voice, deep and resonant, echoed through the forest, sending a shiver of excitement down their spines.

"Greetings, travelers," the voice intoned, its voice carrying the weight of ages. "What brings you to my ancient watch?"

The children stood in shock, their eyes wide with wonder as they looked up at the statue. Its features, once static and unchanging, now seemed to convey a sense of consciousness and presence, as if the figure had been waiting for them all along. The forest around them seemed to hold its breath, amplifying the surreal moment.

Elena gathered all her courage and said, "Greetings. We seek to continue on the trail and find our way back home."

"You seek passage through these ancient lands," the guardian intoned. "To earn your way forward, you must engage in a game of wit and skill. I present to you 'The Riddle of the Elements.'"

"To pass this way," the guardian continued, "you must present the essence of the Earth in three distinct forms. Seek and bring me the following:

1. A leaf from the oldest tree in this forest, whose branches touch the heavens.

2. A stone imbued with the darkest depth of the earth, found where the sunlight seldom reaches.

3. A drop of the purest form of water source blessed by the forest's heart.

Fail in this quest, and you shall be lost within these woods."

Suddenly the path in front of them disappeared.

The children exchanged nervous glances, the gravity of the guardian's challenge sinking in. The enormity of the quest ahead was daunting.

Elena looked around, her brow furrowed with concern. "These questions require a deep understanding of the forest, and we are new here. We don't know the answers." she said, her voice tinged with a sense of worry.

The Guardian remained unmoving, its stone facial expression fixed in an eternal watchfulness. The silence that followed was heavy, amplifying the sense of urgency and uncertainty among the group. The children knew they had to find a way to solve the riddle, but the enormity of the task seemed overwhelming given their lack of knowledge about the forest.

CHAPTER ELEVEN

COMPANIONS IN CHALLENGE

All three of them started to panic, feeling the weight of the seemingly impossible challenge.

Mira looked around anxiously, her voice trembling. "Guys!! What should we do? This challenge seems impossible to solve."

Xavier, his eyes welling with tears, shook his head in despair. "I have no idea. I think we're going to be lost in this forest forever!"

Elena, struggling to keep her composure, took a deep breath and tried to calm the others. "Guys!! Don't panic. Let's sit for a while and think this through."

She guided them to a nearby spot where they could gather their thoughts, hoping that a moment of calm would help them find a solution.

Elena repeated the first riddle aloud, her voice steady despite the situation. "A leaf from the oldest tree in this forest, whose branches touch the heavens."

Mira frowned, trying to piece together the clue. "We need to find the oldest tree, which also seems to be the tallest in the forest."

Xavier, deep in thought, raised a concern. "Even if we manage to find the tallest tree, how will we get a leaf? The fallen leaves could belong to any tree. We might need to wait for the tree to shed a leaf."

Elena and Mira exchanged worried looks, the challenge of the riddle becoming even more daunting. They understood that finding the tree was just the first step; getting a leaf would require patience and perhaps more luck.

Elena recited the second riddle, her voice reflecting her concern. "A stone imbued with the darkest depth of the earth, found where the sunlight seldom reaches."

Mira pondered the riddle's meaning. "It sounds like it's pointing to a place where sunlight doesn't reach, maybe a cave or a deep crevice in the ground."

Xavier's eyes widened with apprehension. "Is it even safe to go to such a place? It could be dangerous, and we don't know what we might encounter in the darkness."

Elena read the third riddle aloud, her voice filled with determination. "A drop of the purest form of water, blessed by the forest's heart."

Mira looked thoughtful. "This suggests that the water must come from a source deeply connected to the forest's essence—perhaps a spring or a hidden pool that's considered sacred or exceptionally clean."

Xavier nodded, adding, "It implies that we need to find a source of water that's not only pure but also significant to the forest, something that embodies the very heart of the forest."

Elena added, "We should look for signs that might lead us to these objects. It might be hidden or revered in some way, so we need to be observant and respect the natural clues we find."

She then suggested, "Let's start with the Guardian's statue. Maybe it holds some clues or hints."

The group agreed and began to examine the statue carefully. They meticulously studied its surface, looking for any carvings, symbols, or hidden compartments that might provide further guidance. They checked every detail, from the intricate textures to the deeper cracks in the stone.

After hours of thorough inspection, their efforts yielded no new information. The statue remained silent and unyielding, its secrets well-guarded.

Suddenly, Mira's attention was drawn back to the squirrel. To her surprise, the little creature had gathered a small assembly of forest friends: birds, squirrels, and even a few rats. They seemed to be forming a curious gathering around the base of the statue, their chatter and rustling drawing the group's gaze.

Elena noticed the commotion and remarked, "Look at that! It seems like the squirrel has attracted quite a crowd. In some way, we could ask them for help!"

Mira's eyes lit up with realization. "That's it! Squirrels can climb trees, birds can fly, and rats can go into the darkest caves. Each of these animals might be able to help us find the items we need for the riddles!"

Xavier, catching on to the idea, added, "We can use their unique abilities to our advantage. Maybe if we guide them or offer them some help, they'll lead us to what we're looking for."

The group gathered around, uncertain about how to proceed with their plan. Elena voiced their collective concern, "But how do we communicate with the animals? How can we ask them for help?"

Just then, they noticed the squirrel rummaging through Mira's bag. Xavier observed, "Maybe he's hungry and looking for some food."

To their astonishment, the squirrel emerged from the bag with a bird-like instrument, the same one they had found in the mysterious room with no door. The sight of the instrument sparked curiosity and confusion among them.

Mira, puzzled, said, "Why would the squirrel be interested in this instrument? Could it be a clue?"

Elena examined the instrument closely. "It's interesting that the squirrel found this. Maybe it's meant to help us communicate with the animals or unlock something we don't understand yet."

"You're right, Elena," Mira said. "I recall seeing similar drawings in the cave, one depicted a girl playing an instrument, and animals gathered around her. Let's give it a try."

Mira brought the whistle to her lips and gave it a blow, but only silence followed, and nothing extraordinary occurred.

"What should we do now?" said Mira.

Elena looked at Mira, concern etched on her face. "It seems like the whistle isn't working. Maybe there's something we're missing."

Mira examined the whistle closely, turning it over in her hands. "Let's check the markings at the bottom again. There might be a clue we're overlooking."

Elena and Xavier peered at the whistle's base, where a symbol was etched. Elena pointed out, "It could be a specific sequence or instruction. If we can figure out what this symbol means, it might help us use the whistle correctly."

Xavier nodded. "If that's the case, maybe the symbol is telling us how to use the whistle in a particular way. It might be about how we blow into it or how we handle it."

Mira examined the whistle again, paying attention to any specific details or instructions that might be implied by the symbol. "Let's try to interpret this. It might be a sequence of notes or a pattern."

Elena added, "Maybe we need to blow into it with a certain rhythm or strength."

Mira took a deep breath and tried a few different approaches, experimenting with varying amounts of air pressure and different rhythms. Despite her efforts, the whistle remained silent, and no magic seemed to happen.

Feeling frustrated but not defeated, Mira said, "I think we're missing something. Perhaps the symbol also indicates a gesture or a specific action we need to perform along with blowing into the whistle."

Just then, they heard the squirrel's excited squeaks, which seemed to be trying to communicate something. The squirrel pointed toward their water bottle and then back at the whistle.

"Guys, I think the squirrel is trying to tell us something," Mira said, catching on. "Look at the symbol on the whistle; it looks like a flowing stream. Maybe it means we need to add water to this top hole."

They carefully poured water into the top hole of the whistle and blew into it. To their astonishment, a loud, melodious chirping sound emerged.

Immediately, all the animals that had gathered around them began to chatter in unison. The squirrel, along with the birds and other creatures, addressed Mira. "How may we assist you, Ms. Mira?"

Mira took a deep breath and addressed the assembled animals. "Can you help us find three things we need?

1. A leaf from the tallest tree in the forest.

2. A stone imbued with the darkest depth of the earth, found where sunlight seldom reaches.

3. A drop of the purest form of water from a source blessed by the forest's heart."

The animals nodded in understanding, ready to assist with their unique abilities.

The animals sprang into action with purpose. The birds took flight, soaring high to search for the tallest tree in the forest and locate its leaf. The rats scurried off, making their way toward the darkest, most shadowed places to find the stone imbued with the earth's depth. Meanwhile, the squirrels darted through the underbrush, heading toward sources of water to find the purest drop blessed by the forest's heart.

The trio waited anxiously, hoping the animals would find the items they needed. As the sun dipped below the horizon, the forest grew dim, and they decided to rest for the night, planning to wait until morning for any updates.

At dawn, they were roused by the cheerful chirping of the birds. Elena, Mira, and Xavier stretched and opened their eyes. To their immense relief, the birds had successfully returned with a vibrant, green leaf from the tallest tree in the forest.

Shortly after, the rats scurried into view, carrying a heavy, dark stone.

However, the squirrels, who had been darting around energetically, returned with empty paws. Their tiny faces reflected frustration and disappointment, and they chattered anxiously amongst themselves.

Elena, Mira, and Xavier gathered together, their initial joy overshadowed by concern. They had successfully obtained two of the three items, but the quest for the purest drop of water remained incomplete.

As they discussed their next steps, Xavier's eyes caught the glimmer of early morning light reflecting off the grass. He pointed excitedly, "Look, guys! Those droplets of water on the grass...the dew... are the purest form of water you can find."

The dewdrops sparkled in the soft morning light, each tiny droplet catching the sun's rays and shimmering like liquid crystal. They were pristine, untouched by the elements, and perfectly pure. Elena, Mira, and Xavier realized that these dewdrops might be the solution they had been searching for.

With newfound hope, they carefully collected the dew in a small leaf, ready to complete the final part of their quest.

After gathering the dewdrops, the trio thanked the animals for their invaluable assistance. The birds, rats, and the squirrels received their gratitude warmly, with the animals chattering and chirping in a symphony of farewell.

However, one particular squirrel lingered behind, its tiny eyes full of determination and curiosity. It seemed reluctant to leave the group. Mira noticed the squirrel's steadfast presence and gently asked, "Would you like to stay with us a bit longer? We're about to face the Guardian again."

The squirrel, with a twitch of its tail, appeared to nod in agreement, as if understanding the gravity of the situation. It scampered alongside them, ready to offer any additional help it could provide.

With their tasks completed, the trio, accompanied by their loyal squirrel companion, made their way back to the Guardian's statue.

The Guardian, still as majestic and imposing as ever, awaited their return. Its carved eyes seemed to follow them as they approached with the leaf, stone, and container of dew. The air around the statue felt charged with anticipation.

Elena, taking a deep breath, stepped forward and presented the items. "O Great Guardian, we have returned with the answers to your riddles. Here is a leaf from the tallest tree in the forest, a stone imbued with the darkest depth, and a drop of the purest water from the forest's heart."

The Guardian's stone-carved face remained impassive for a moment, but then a deep, resonant voice filled the air. "You have fulfilled the challenge with wisdom and perseverance. Your offerings are true and pure. The forest acknowledges your efforts.

CHAPTER TWELVE

THE BOON OF THE GODDESS

As soon as the Guardian accepted the offerings, the trail reappeared, leading them forward. However, their relief was short-lived as they faced a new obstacle, the path now passed through a pink river, its surface shimmering with an otherworldly glow.

Xavier, staring at the river with concern, turned to the others. "How should we cross the river?"

Before anyone could respond, the Guardian's stone face softened into an expression of assurance. "I shall carry you on my shoulder," the Guardian declared, his voice resonating with a deep, comforting tone.

With a thunderous sound, the Guardian's statue began to move. The ground trembled as the massive figure slowly stood up. Its movements were slow but deliberate, and its stone joints creaked as it took its first step.

Mira watched in awe as the Guardian approached the river, its immense form casting a protective shadow over them. "This is incredible," she said, her voice filled with both relief and amazement.

The Guardian bent down, extending its broad shoulder towards the trio. "Climb aboard," it instructed.

Elena, Mira, and Xavier carefully ascended onto the Guardian's shoulder, with squirrel over Mira's shoulder, holding tightly as the figure began to walk towards the river. The pink water lapped gently at the edges of the riverbank, reflecting a spectrum of colors.

As they approached the river, the Guardian waded into the shimmering water. Despite the ethereal appearance of the river, the Guardian's immense strength made the crossing seem effortless. The pink water splashed around them, creating a mesmerizing display of colors as they progressed through the river.

Xavier glanced at the squirrel who had decided to follow them. "Looks like this squirrel has decided to stay with us," he said with a smile. "He's one of us now. Should we give him a name?"

Elena and Mira nodded in agreement. "What shall we name him?" Mira asked, looking at the small creature with curiosity.

After a moment of thought, Elena suggested, "How about Angel? He's been our Guardian angel. Without him, we might still be lost in this forest."

Xavier's face lit up with a smile. "I think Angel is a perfect name for him."

The trio watched as Angel, the squirrel, squeaked with what seemed to be excitement. He twitched his tail and scampered around in circles, clearly pleased with his new name.

"Angel it is then," Mira said, reaching out to give the squirrel a gentle pat.

Once they reached the far side of the river, the Guardian gently set them down on solid ground. "You have now crossed the river safely," the Guardian said, its voice echoing with a hint of satisfaction.

The trio expressed their gratitude, their voices filled with relief and appreciation. "Thank you so much for your help," Elena said, her eyes reflecting her gratitude.

The Guardian nodded solemnly in response, its stone facial expression showing a flicker of warmth. Without another word, he turned and began to walk towards a nearby temple, its imposing figure fading into the distance.

Mira, Xavier, and Elena exchanged glances, their faces a mix of curiosity and apprehension. The sight of the temple—a structure partially concealed by the dense forest and bathed in a soft, golden light—stirred their sense of wonder.

"We should follow him," Mira said, her voice steady despite the underlying uncertainty. "The Guardian might be leading us to something important."

Xavier nodded in agreement. "Yes, we don't know what's in the temple, but it could be another crucial part of our journey."

Elena looked at Angel, who was scampering excitedly around them. "And we have our new friend Angel with us. He's been such a help so far."

With a collective nod, the trio set off towards the temple, Angel darting ahead and then pausing to make sure they were following. As they approached the temple, the forest seemed to quieten, creating an atmosphere of reverence and anticipation.

The temple's entrance was framed by ancient stone pillars, adorned with intricate carvings and overgrown with vines. It stood as a silent guardian of secrets and mysteries.

With a deep breath, Elena pushed open the heavy doors of the temple. The creaking of the ancient wood and the faint scent of incense greeted them as they stepped inside, their eyes adjusting to the dim light.

The interior of the temple was vast and filled with echoes. Sunlight streamed through high windows, casting ethereal patterns on the stone floor.

As the trio stepped further into the temple, they saw the Guardian kneeling before a small statue of a goddess. The statue was intricately carved, depicting a serene deity surrounded by symbols of nature—leaves, flowers, and flowing water. The atmosphere in the temple seemed to grow even more solemn and worshipful.

The Guardian's voice, though still deep and resonant, carried a note of weariness. "Oh, Goddess of the Forest," he intoned, "I have brought what I was asked for. Please relieve me from my duty."

With a careful, worshipful motion, the Guardian presented the elements that the trio had previously offered him. The leaf from the tallest tree, the dark stone, and the container of dew. He placed them gently before the goddess's statue, his large hands shaking slightly from the weight of his responsibility.

The trio watched in silence, feeling a profound sense of curiosity. The Guardian's dedication and solemnity underscored the importance of the moment. As the Guardian finished his plea, he slowly stood, his stone form seeming to sag with relief.

The goddess's statue, though immobile and silent, appeared to shimmer subtly, as if acknowledging the Guardian's request. A gentle breeze stirred within the temple, carrying with it the faint scent of blooming flowers and fresh rain.

Elena, Mira, and Xavier stood by, their hearts filled with anticipation. They understood that this moment was significant not only for the Guardian but also for their own quest. They waited, holding their breath, as the air seemed to hold its own quiet aura.

The goddess's presence, though unseen, felt palpable. The trio sensed a shift in the atmosphere, as if the temple itself was responding to the Guardian's offering and request.

After a moment of stillness, the Guardian's statue seemed to emit a soft glow. The light enveloped the room, bathing the trio and the goddess's statue in a warm, golden hue. The glow was gentle but filled with a profound sense of peace and fulfillment.

The Guardian looked at the trio, his eyes reflecting a mixture of gratitude and newfound freedom. "Thank you for aiding me in this task," he said, his voice now carrying a tone of relief. "My duty is complete, and I am finally free."

The Guardian began to shrink, his massive stone form diminishing rapidly. Within moments, the imposing giant sculpture transformed into a young man. Standing where the colossal figure had been, was a human figure, clothed in simple yet elegant garments that seemed to blend harmoniously with the forest's natural hues.

The man, who had once been the Guardian, looked both relieved and serene. His presence was now more approachable, yet still carried an air of wisdom and authority. He gave the trio a warm, appreciative smile.

The man began to speak, his voice now gentle and kind. "My name is Magnus Ravenswood. Thank you for helping me to be freed from my curse," he said with a deep, heartfelt gratitude. "I was cursed by a witch in this forest to be a stone man. Every day, I prayed to the goddess of the forest for relief. Finally, she asked me to procure these items, promising that she would lift the curse if I succeeded. But there was a condition: I was not allowed to move from my place until I had gathered these things."

Magnus's eyes glistened with emotion as he continued. "Until now, I had encountered many travelers, but none were able to help me. Your determination and courage have finally broken the curse, and I am free."

He took a deep breath, the weight of his past burden seeming to lift with his words. "I am eternally grateful to you."

Elena, Mira, and Xavier approached Magnus with a mixture of curiosity and respect. Elena spoke for the group, saying, "You're welcome. We're glad we could help. What happens now?"

Magnus looked thoughtful for a moment, his eyes reflecting both relief and determination. "Now, I must continue my journey as well, to return to where I belong. If you're willing, I would be honored to join you for the path ahead. My knowledge of the forest and its secrets could be of great assistance to you."

Elena, Mira, and Xavier exchanged glances, considering the offer. They could see the sincerity in Magnus's eyes and understood the value of having someone with his experience accompany them.

Mira nodded first, her voice filled with optimism. "I think having you with us would be very helpful. Your knowledge of the forest could be invaluable."

Xavier agreed, adding, "And it would be great to have another experienced traveler on our side. We could use all the help we can get."

Elena smiled warmly. "Welcome to our journey, Magnus. We're glad to have you with us."

Magnus's face lit up with a genuine smile. "Thank you. I look forward to traveling with you and assisting in any way I can."

With their new companion joining them, the group felt a renewed sense of unity and strength. As they prepared to set out, they knew that the path ahead would be filled with new challenges, but with Magnus's guidance, they were ready to face whatever came their way.

Suddenly, a soft, resonant voice filled the temple, and the voice emerged from the statue of the goddess. " Magnus, you have served the forest faithfully through your trials. As a reward for your dedication, I bestow upon you this compass. It will guide you in the right direction when the path is lost." As she spoke, a beautifully crafted compass materialized before them, its surface shimmering with a subtle, otherworldly light. The group rejoiced over the blessing, their spirits lifted by the divine gift. They thanked the goddess and continued their journey.

97

CHAPTER THIRTEEN

TALE OF THE GUARDIAN

With Magnus now leading the way, the group continued their journey through the forest. Magnus, with his knowledge of the land, navigated with confidence, his steps purposeful and sure.

"No matter what," Magnus said firmly, "we must stay on the path. Losing it means we'll be lost forever."

Elena, Mira, Xavier and Angel nodded in agreement, understanding the importance of maintaining their course. They kept their eyes on the trail, knowing that any misstep could lead them into unknown and potentially dangerous territory.

Magnus glanced back, curiosity in his eyes. "How did a group of children like you end up in this forest?"

Mira, Xavier, and Elena shared their story: How they had been on a school trip when a mysterious wall had pulled them into a room with no doors. Solving the riddle had been their only way out.

Magnus listened intently, his eyes widening as he absorbed their tale. "So you were brought here by pure chance, driven by your curiosity and determination. It's remarkable that you've made it this far and managed to solve the riddles," he said, his voice filled with a mix of admiration.

"You've not only shown great courage but also a heart full of purity and resolve," Magnus added, nodding appreciatively. "Your journey through the forest and the challenges you've faced are truly extraordinary."

Magnus glanced at the group again with a hint of hesitation. "How is the Onyx Panther Dynasty?" he asked, his tone laced with genuine curiosity.

"The what?" The trio responded in unison, clearly puzzled by the unfamiliar name.

"The Onyx Panther Dynasty," Magnus repeated, his gaze thoughtful.

The group exchanged curious looks, eager to learn more. "What can you tell us about it?" Mira asked, leaning in slightly.

Magnus began recounting the dynasty's legacy. "The Onyx Panther Dynasty was ruled by King Aric Onyx Panther. The capital city, Nocturna, was renowned for its prosperity and cultural achievements. Under King Aric's reign, the region flourished, distinguished by its advancements in art, architecture, and trade. Nocturna was a city of grand palaces and bustling markets, reflecting the grandeur and importance of the dynasty."

Elena's eyes widened with interest. "That sounds fascinating.

"I read about it in a history book. It was a significant dynasty that existed about 200 years ago," said Xavier.

"It seems like you were stuck here for a very long time," Elena remarked. "In the world we come from, there are no dynasties like The Onyx Panther Dynasty. We have nations where people choose their leaders through elections and other democratic processes."

Magnus was puzzled by this new revelation. "I initially believed it had been only 10 to 15 years," he sighed, "but in reality, I was trapped as a stone figure for nearly 200 years."

Elena noticed the deep sorrow in Magnus's eyes and felt a pang of empathy. She stepped closer, her voice gentle and reassuring.

"I can only imagine how difficult it must have been for you," Elena said softly. "Two hundred years is an unimaginable length of time to be trapped in one place. But you've shown incredible strength and perseverance through all of it.

She placed a comforting hand on Magnus's shoulder, offering a sincere smile. "Your story and your actions have led us here. You've protected the forest and its secrets, and that's something truly remarkable."

Magnus nodded and zoned out, and the group fell into a thoughtful silence. After a moment, Mira broke the quiet, her voice gentle but curious. "Can you tell us your story, Sir? How did you come to be in this place?"

Magnus blinked as if coming out of a trance, then began to recount his tale.

"Many years ago," Magnus began, his voice heavy with the weight of old regrets, "a legend spoke of an incredibly precious treasure hidden deep within this forest. The tales of its power and riches attracted countless adventurers, but none ever returned.

I was from the village where this cave exists, and the elders knew well that there was nothing but danger within its depths. As a result, none of us villagers ever set foot inside.

But at the time, I was a soldier in The Onyx Panther Dynasty. The king, troubled by these mysterious disappearances, summoned me and a few other soldiers to uncover the truth behind them. I tried to reason with the king, suggesting that we should seal the cave to prevent anyone else from entering. But he dismissed my concerns. So, my comrades and I ventured into the cave to uncover the truth."

He paused, his eyes clouded with the weight of his memories. "As we ventured deeper into the forest, we stumbled upon a chilling revelation. We encountered a treasure hunter who had been wandering lost within the forest. He told us that it was the king himself who had been sending people into the forest, fully aware of the dangers that lay within. The king's true aim was to find the treasure and keep it for himself, regardless of the lives lost in the process."

Magnus's voice grew somber, laced with a sense of betrayal. "Realizing the king's treachery, we found ourselves at a crossroads. We knew we had to stop him and protect the people from coming inside this forest, but our loyalty was conflicted. The king's orders were unyielding, yet we couldn't ignore the wrongs we had uncovered. Torn between duty and justice, we decided to take matters into our own hands."

He looked at the trio with a mix of resolve and regret. "But before we could act, disaster struck. We lost all our companions. Some were devoured by wild beasts lurking in the shadows, while others were swept away by the river's treacherous currents. I was left alone, overwhelmed and heartbroken. I strayed from the path, forgetting the dire warnings. I stumbled into a cursed vine—an ancient enchantment upon touching it the path disappeared. After that, no matter how hard I searched, the path eluded me."

Magnus's gaze grew distant, his expression reflecting the depth of his despair. "As I wandered aimlessly through the forest, I encountered a witch. She was like the forest itself, with eyes that seemed to hold all its secrets. Enraged by my trespassing and my failure to follow the path, she declared that I had no place in her domain. In her wrath, she cursed me to remain a stone forever, bound to this place as a reminder of my failure."

Magnus's voice grew soft with a hint of desperation. "Every day, I prayed to the forest goddess, pleading with her to understand my true intentions. I never sought the treasure for myself; my only desire was to help those who had become lost in these woods. I wanted to make things right, to protect the innocents from the king's deceit and the dangers of the forest. I implored her to see the sincerity of my heart and to free me from my curse."

He continued, his tone laden with emotion, "The goddess finally answered my prayers, but she set a task before me. Over the years, I stood at the trail, waiting for someone to solve the riddles and assist me. Yet, the same fate awaited everyone—none ever returned. But finally, you three kids have achieved what others could not. Your hearts must be truly pure," he said, pausing as if overwhelmed by the weight of his words.

The group listened, captivated by the blend of intrigue and tragedy in Magnus's story.

Elena said, "So this must be why the cave was closed. Whoever did it didn't want anyone else to get lost in these woods. But now that the cave has been reopened, the disappearances have started again, and we're the first victims."

Magus replied, "Whoever sealed the cave did the right thing. Over the years, I've noticed that the number of visitors to the forest has steadily declined. You must be the first ones to come here in a long time."

The forest, once a realm of mystery, now felt overwhelmingly sinister. Shadows moved with unsettling intensity, and the air was thick with ominous silence. Each creak and rustle seemed to echo the forest's forgotten secrets. What was once merely foreboding now felt like a living entity, watching and waiting, as if the reopening of the cave had awakened something ancient and dangerous within the woods.

CHAPTER FOURTEEN

LOST AND REDISCOVERED

After hearing the words of Magnus the trio were more frightened than before, the group decided to proceed with heightened caution. They gathered together to discuss the potential dangers that might lie ahead, their voices tinged with anxiety.

"Magnus," Elena asked, "Can you please tell us more about this witch?"

Magnus's expression grew serious again, his voice carrying a blend of fright and caution. "Ah, the witch," he began. "She is indeed a figure of both formidable and enigmatic. This Enchanted Forest is her domain, and she guards it with a fierce protectiveness that most can scarcely imagine.

Her magic is unlike anything you'll find in common lore. It is deeply intertwined with the essence of the forest itself. She's less of a traditional witch and more of a guardian spirit, bound to the land and its secrets."

Elena and the others listened intently, their anticipation mingling with a hint of apprehension

"The witch has been safeguarding something within this forest for centuries," Magnus continued. "No one has ever been able to uncover exactly what it is. The mystery of her protection is part of what makes her so formidable.

Let's hope we don't cross her path," Magnus added with a grave tone. "If she discovers us trespassing, the consequences could be severe. The forest is her realm, and her wrath is not to be taken lightly."

The group nodded, and their pace quickened unintentionally.

"So, Magus," Elena asked thoughtfully, her brow furrowed in concern, "do you think it could be her doing—the cave, the trap room, the wishing well? Why would she help us with wishing well if she's so bad?"

"As per the old stories," Magnus explained, his voice carrying the weight of history, "the barrier between our world and this one was created by a powerful wizard from the village. It was intended to be a secret, allowing only a select few to cross into this realm. However, over time, the knowledge of how to navigate the cave and enter this world became less guarded. As a result, treasure hunters began to venture into this realm, driven by tales of its hidden riches."

"According to me," Magnus continued, his tone thoughtful, "the rest of what we've encountered, the traps, the hidden room, and even the seemingly helpful elements like the wishing well, must be the work of the witch. It seems she has taken it upon herself to protect the forest and keep intruders at bay. Her actions are likely aimed at preventing anyone from entering too deeply into her domain."

"But wishing well?" Mira asked again, clearly puzzled.

"Don't you get it?" Xavier replied, his tone brightening with realization. "Not many people would want to leave wishing well after being stuck in the hidden room for days. The wishing well might have seemed like a perfect place to settle down for those who found it. It offers a semblance of comfort and hope. Remember, not many people would be able to leave, And even you Mira considered staying there for a while."

Mira's eyes widened as she processed Xavier's explanation. A look of understanding mixed with concern crossed her face. "So, you're saying that the wishing well was designed to trap people by offering them a false sense of hope?" she asked, her voice tinged with realization.

Elena nodded slowly, her expression thoughtful. "It makes sense. The well could be a way for the witch to control and manipulate those who find themselves lost or desperate, making them believe they have a chance to escape while actually keeping them trapped. It's both clever and sinister."

Both Mira and Elena took a moment to absorb the implication. Mira, still processing, looked more determined. "We need to stay sharp and not be fooled by any more illusions or traps. The witch is clearly very powerful and elusive."

Magnus nodded, clearly impressed by their insight. "You're absolutely right," he said, his voice tinged with admiration. "Your understanding of the situation is spot-on. The wishing well was indeed a clever trap, designed to deceive and contain those who stumbled upon it. Your ability to see through the witch's manipulations is remarkable."

He paused, clearly stunned by their smartness. "I underestimated your resourcefulness. We must remain vigilant and use this knowledge to our advantage as we move forward."

After hours of safe travel, the group decided to rest for a while and found a perfect spot for resting.

Mira shared the fruits she had gathered from the wishing well with Magnus and Angel. "We only have enough food for a day," she said, her voice tinged with worry.

"Don't worry; we'll gather some fruits along the way," Magnus reassured them. The team nodded in relief.

Just then, a stunning butterfly fluttered down and landed gently on Mira's hand. Captivated by its beauty, Mira watched in awe as it danced on her palm before taking flight. "Don't go!" she cried, instinctively running after it.

"Watch out!" Magnus warned, but it was too late. As Mira reached out to follow the butterfly, her hand brushed against a vine. Instantly, the path before them began to disappear, and the ground shifted beneath their feet.

"Oh no!" the group shouted in panic and despair.

Mira began to cry, her face flushed with shame and fear. "What have I done? Now we'll be lost in this forest forever. What if the witch finds us?" she sobbed.

"Don't cry," Elena said gently, her voice filled with reassurance. "We need to stay calm and find a solution. There must be a way out of this. Let's work together and figure it out." The rest of the group nodded in agreement, rallying around Mira to offer their support and to brainstorm their next steps.

Suddenly, a smile broke across Mira's face as she remembered something. "What about the compass given by the goddess?" she exclaimed. "It's supposed to guide us in the right direction when the path is lost!"

The group's expressions brightened with hope. Magus quickly retrieved the compass from his pocket, holding it up for everyone to see. The needle inside spun for a moment before it settled, pointing steadily in a specific direction.

"Looks like it wants us to go in that direction!" Xavier said, pointing at the compass. The group carefully began to walk in the direction indicated by the needle.

After several hours of trekking, they finally glimpsed a majestic mountain rising in the distance. Its jagged peaks, partially hidden by swirling, misty clouds, loomed like ancient guards stood there guarding the forest. The mountain's base was shrouded in dense fog, giving the impression that it emerged from the earth itself, towering into the heavens.

"Look at that mountain," Elena said, pointing toward the towering peak. "The compass is directing us toward it. We might have to climb that as part of our journey."

Magnus nodded gravely. "According to folk tales from the village, the witch is said to reside in a mountain described just like this one. "

The group exchanged uneasy glances, their earlier relief quickly overshadowed by a new wave of apprehension. Elena's eyes widened with concern, and she tightened her grip on her pack. Mira looked nervously at the dense forest around them.

Xavier took a deep breath and nodded resolutely, trying to steady his nerves. "We'll have to stay alert and stick together," he said, attempting to sound more confident than he felt.

Angel, usually quiet, broke the silence with a determined expression and squeaked positively. As if he meant, "We can do this. We've come this far and faced challenges before. Let's stay focused and make sure we're ready for whatever comes next."

The group nodded in agreement. "Another day has passed; we should rest before continuing our journey in the morning," Elena announced.

They found a nearby cave and decided to spend the night there. As they settled in, the cave provided a brief respite from the eerie forest and the looming mountain.

CHAPTER FIFTEEN

LION AND THE FRUIT

After talking for a couple of hours, the group gradually fell asleep, exhausted from their tedious journey. The cave, though cold and dimly lit, provided a welcome shelter from the eerie forest and looming mountain outside. One by one, their tired bodies found rest, the crackling campfire casting flickering shadows on the walls as they drifted into a deep, much-needed slumber.

Suddenly, everyone was jolted awake by Angel's urgent warning. Their hearts raced as they blinked into the dim light of the cave. Angel's voice was sharp and filled with panic.

"A lion!" Elena shouted, pointing toward the cave entrance.

The group scrambled to their feet, their sleepiness instantly replaced by fear. The shadow of a massive lion loomed in the entrance, its golden eyes gleaming ominously in the low light. The creature's muscular frame and menacing growl sent shivers down their spines.

Elena grabbed a nearby branch, holding it defensively as she scanned for any potential escape routes. Mira, wide-eyed with terror, clung to her pack. Magnus, usually calm under pressure, quickly assessed the situation, trying to get their act together.

"Stay calm!" Magnus instructed, though his own voice betrayed his concern. "We need to think fast. The cave must belong to the lion".

Xavier, his mind racing, suggested, "We need to find a way to either scare it off or find another exit. If we can't fight it, we'll have to outsmart it."

The group, hearts pounding, readied themselves to face the formidable beast. Each member prepared in their own way—Elena with her branch, Xavier with a plan to distract the lion, and Magnus trying to figure out the best course of action to ensure their safety.

As the lion's growls grew louder and its massive paws edged closer, the team knew they had to act swiftly if they were to escape this new danger.

Suddenly, Elena's voice cut through the tension. "Mira! The whistle! Keep it ready!"

Mira's eyes widened as she recalled the small, bird shaped whistle. She scrambled through her bag, her hands shaking, until she found it. With a nod of determination, she filled the whistle with water.

"Got it!" Mira shouted back, her voice steady despite her fear.

Just before the lion could pounce on the distressed Angel, Mira blew the whistle with all her strength. The sharp, chirping sound filled the cave, cutting through the tension.

The lion halted in its tracks, its powerful muscles tensing as it turned its head toward Mira. Its golden eyes locked onto her, and to everyone's astonishment, the ferocious beast began to calm down, its stance shifting from aggressive to relaxed. A deep, rumbling purr, almost like that of a large cat, emanated from its chest.

The group watched in stunned silence as the lion, now noticeably less menacing, settled on its haunches and waited expectantly for Mira's command. The transformation from a threatening predator to a seemingly obedient creature was nothing short of remarkable.

Mira, with a newfound sense of authority, addressed the lion with a calm but commanding voice. "Stay here and guard the entrance until morning." The lion, understanding the seriousness in her tone, settled down in front of the cave entrance, its watchful eyes scanning the surroundings.

Turning back to the group, Mira said with a reassuring tone, "Now we can all go back to sleep. We don't have to take turns watching over the cave; the lion will guard us until morning."

Magnus's curiosity was piqued. "Where did you find this whistle?" he asked, his eyes narrowing with interest.

Mira looked at him and explained, "We found it hidden in that room. We figured out how to use it while solving the riddles given by you."

Magnus nodded thoughtfully, clearly impressed. "It seems we've stumbled upon a very useful tool. We should keep it handy from now on. This whistle could be crucial in protecting us from the wild beasts of this region. The Enchanted Forest is known for its dangerous and unpredictable wildlife."

Elena, overhearing the conversation, added, "It's good that we have it. Given the dangers ahead, it's better to be prepared for anything."

The team went back to sleep, feeling safe as the lion guarded the cave.

Once morning arrived, the lion gave a deep, resonant roar and, true to its word, left the cave. The sound echoed through the forest, signaling the start of a new day. The team, roused from their sleep, stirred groggily but with a renewed sense of security.

Mira, Elena, Magnus, Xavier, and Angel began to prepare for their journey ahead. They gathered their belongings, and took a moment to stretch their stiff muscles. The previous night's ordeal had left them weary, but the sight of the lion's departure and the promise of a new day invigorated their spirits.

With their rumbling stomach and path set, the team left the cave, ready to face whatever the Enchanted Forest and the looming mountain had in store for them.

As they headed towards the mountain, they found a tree full of purple fruits. The team ran towards the tree hoping they could get their hands on some of the fruits.

Suddenly Angel started to squeak loudly.

"Guys, I don't recognize this fruit. We probably shouldn't eat it!" Magnus suggested, his voice filled with concern as he examined a strange, vibrant fruit he had come across.

However, Xavier, driven by hunger and curiosity, had already taken a bite before Magnus's warning had fully sunk in. At first, he savored the sweetness, but then a strange tingling sensation began to spread through his body.

Suddenly, Xavier's eyes widened in surprise as his body started to undergo a bizarre transformation. His arms and legs began to shrink, and his clothes seemed to grow larger around him. In a matter of moments, Xavier had turned into a small, chubby squirrel, his eyes wide with a mix of confusion and alarm.

The group stared in disbelief as the now tiny Xavier scampered around the cave, his tiny paws waving frantically. His attempts to communicate were reduced to high-pitched squeaks and frantic gestures.

Mira burst into laughter, despite the seriousness of their situation. "Xavier, you're a squirrel!" she exclaimed, trying to stifle her giggles.

Elena, her concern quickly replaced by amusement, said, "Well, that's one way to avoid being hungry!"

Magnus, though initially worried, couldn't help but chuckle at the sight of Xavier's furry antics. "It looks like the fruit has some unexpected side effects. We'll need to find a way to reverse this."

Xavier, now thoroughly bewildered, attempted to climb up a rock, only to tumble back down in a comical heap. The sight of him scurrying about with a tiny, fluffy tail and twitching nose added an element of humor to their situation.

Magnus, still chuckling, added, "Let's search the forest for any herbs or items that could reverse this transformation. We need to help Xavier return to his normal self. Over the years, I've learned that for every problem caused by the forest, there's often a solution hidden within it. We just need to look for it with patience."

The group, now more hopeful, spread out cautiously to search the surrounding forest. They kept their eyes peeled for any clues, magical herbs, or peculiar items that might assist in their quest. The forest was dense and full of surprises, but Magnus's words gave them renewed determination.

As they continued their search, Mira inched closer to Elena and asked quietly, "Elena, are you thinking what I'm thinking?"

Elena looked at her curiously and nodded. "What if we can't find something that can reverse Xavier's spell?"

Mira's face reflected a mix of concern and curiosity. "Oh! I was thinking—what if Angel was also transformed by the fruit?"

Elena paused, considering Mira's words. After a moment, she shook her head. "That's impossible. Magnus mentioned that no one has visited this forest for a long time. If Angel had been a human once, he would have been dead by now."

Mira frowned, realizing the implications. "You're right. If Angel had been transformed, he wouldn't have survived for so long."

Meanwhile Magnus's thoughts raced as he connected the dots. "It makes sense," he said aloud. "If the purple fruit turned Xavier into a squirrel, then finding something with the opposite color might help reverse the effect."

The group approached the tree with the bright yellow fruits hanging from its branches. Elena eyed the fruits cautiously. "Do you really think these will work?" she asked, her voice tinged with both hope and skepticism.

Magnus nodded. "In theory, yes. If the yellow fruit is indeed the complementary color of the purple fruit, it might counteract the spell. But we should be careful. We don't know for sure how it will work."

Mira carefully picked one of the yellow fruits and inspected it. It looked vibrant and inviting, but they needed to be sure before taking any risks. "Should we test it first, maybe on something smaller or less risky?" she suggested.

Elena agreed, suggesting they use a small piece of the fruit or perhaps test it on something non-living if they could find it. "We should be cautious," she said. "If it doesn't work or causes another problem, we want to minimize the risk."

As the team debated the safest course of action, they spotted a small, fallen dry twig on the ground. They decided to test a small piece of the yellow fruit on it first. Magnus carefully scraped a bit of the fruit's pulp onto the twig.

The group watched anxiously as the twig sat still for a few moments. Nothing happened at first, but then the twig began to glow faintly before returning to life with its normal appearance. It was promising, but they needed to see more substantial results.

With the small test seeming successful, they decided to move forward with their plan. Mira turned to Xavier, who was still in the squirrel form. "We're going to give you some of this yellow fruit. Hopefully, it will reverse the transformation."

Mira held a piece of the yellow fruit in her hand and approached Xavier cautiously. She gently offered it to him. Xavier, the squirrel sniffed the fruit curiously before taking a small bite.

As soon as the fruit touched his mouth, a shimmering glow enveloped Xavier. Slowly but surely, his furry form began to change. The transformation reversed, and soon Xavier was back to his human self, much to everyone's relief and delight.

The group cheered as Xavier, now fully restored, looked around in amazement. "That worked better than I expected," he said with a grin. However, Angel remained quiet, a hint of hesitation on his face.

Magnus smiled, clearly relieved and pleased with the outcome. "Well done, everyone. It seems the complementary color theory worked after all. Let's keep this fruit with us just in case we need it again."

Mira, driven by her curiosity and the need to confirm her suspicions, cautiously pushed a piece of the yellow fruit toward Angel. She held her breath, watching intently as the Angel the squirrel ate the fruit.

In a matter of moments, the glow enveloped Angel completely, and where the squirrel had stood, there now appeared a beautiful young girl. She had long, flowing hair and a graceful, ethereal presence, with features that reflected both strength and kindness.

CHAPTER SIXTEEN

ANGEL IS A GIRL

Stunned by the sudden and unexpected transformation, the team stood there, dumbstruck. Their eyes widened in disbelief as they tried to process the shocking revelation before them. The air seemed to hold its breath, amplifying the silence that enveloped the group. Each member's face reflected a mix of astonishment, confusion, and growing curiosity as they struggled to reconcile the newfound reality with the familiar person they had known for so long.

Xavier's eyes widened in shock, and he exclaimed, "Wait, Angel is a girl?!"

The girl blinked, her eyes adjusting to the surroundings, and looked around with a mixture of confusion and recognition. Her gaze settled on the group, and she smiled warmly.

Mira gasped in astonishment, "Angel... is that really you?"

The girl nodded, her voice now clear and melodious. "Yes, it's me. Thank you for freeing me from that form. I was transformed long ago and had lost hope of ever returning to my true self."

The group stood in stunned silence, processing the revelation. Elena stepped forward, her face showing a mix of relief and curiosity.

"How did this happen? Magnus mentioned that no one had been here for a long time."

Angel, now fully revealed, regarded them with a contemplative gaze. "Many years ago, I was transformed after eating fruit from this very tree. It appears that the spell could only be undone by an object of complementary color to the original enchantment. I have been trapped in this form, patiently awaiting someone to come to my aid. But it's true that no one set foot into this forest in this century."

"I tried to warn you not to eat that fruit, but Xavier went ahead and did it anyway," Angel said, her voice tinged with relief and uncertainty. "Thanks to him and Mira, I could return to my true self. For a while, I was in shock. I had been to this part of the forest many times, something I had been searching for all these years was right here, but I never imagined these fruits to be curative of my curse. And for a while I started to think if I should really return to my human form. But the moment Mira gave me the fruit, I regained my senses. And also thanks to Magnus he was able to figure out the solution in no time."

Magnus, though still shocked from earlier, was now deeply interested. "It seems the fruit indeed worked as we hoped. This is quite a discovery."

Elena's curiosity grew as Angel shared her story. "But how did you survive all these years?" she asked, her voice filled with both compassion and intrigue.

Angel took a deep breath, her eyes reflecting the weight of her past experiences. "I reached out to the witch in this forest, I begged her to reverse the spell, to turn me back into a human. But she only laughed at my misery and dismissed me. She told me that the consequences of trespassing were mine to bear and that only the forest could relieve me from my curse."

Angel's gaze grew distant as she continued, "Determined to find a way out, I followed her for a while. I discovered a particular tree she visited every full moon. She consumed the fruits of this tree, which allowed her to remain alive for centuries. I, too, ate those fruits, hoping they would hold the key to lifting my curse so that I could return home. But despite my efforts, I never figured out how to break the spell."

Mira, intrigued by Angel's tale, asked, "Do you have any idea why the witch's magic is so powerful, or if there were any other clues she might have left behind?"

Angel shook her head. "The witch is elusive and enigmatic. She left no clear clues, only her disrespect and the magical fruit. I was left with nothing but hope and the occasional appearance of the witch, which was never long enough to gather any useful information."

Angel's revelation added a new layer of mystery to their quest. Her expression was a mix of hope and frustration as she shared her experience.

"How did you find the witch, do you know where she lives"? asked Xavier.

"One day, I managed to find the witch in the forest and followed her," Angel began. "I have discovered that she has a secret entrance somewhere in the mountains. However, the entrance is hidden and becomes almost impossible to track as time passes. The witch knows how to cover her tracks, making it nearly impossible to follow her for long."

Xavier, absorbed in the details, asked, "So, what's the plan if we want to find this secret entrance?"

Angel continued, "The only reliable way to locate her is to wait near the mountain on a full moon night. That's when the entrance becomes accessible. But be warned—during that time, almost all the animals in the vicinity stand guard. It's incredibly difficult to get close, let alone enter the witch's domain."

Magnus looked thoughtful. "We need a strategy for that night. If we're to approach the witch's secret entrance, we'll need a plan to avoid detection and navigate through the guards."

Then Elena said, "Our goal should be to reach home without being detected by the witch. Let's worry about that first."

Mira asked with a bit of hesitation "So, Angel, what is your name?".

Angel, her eyes bright with a mixture of gratitude and relief, said, "I'm so sorry I didn't introduce myself earlier. My name is Selene, but you can call me Angel. It's a name you gave me, and it symbolizes my newfound freedom, so I cherish it."

Mira smiled warmly at Angel, nodding in agreement. "It suits you perfectly."

Angel's expression became more animated as she continued, "Over the years, I've learned a lot about this forest. There's a spring nearby whose water has a special property—it can reveal the hidden path and make them visible again. Plus, the area around it is abundant with edible fruits, which could really help us regain our strength."

Her eyes twinkled with a hopeful gleam. "I can lead you there. It's a place where we can rest, eat, and rejuvenate."

The group followed Angel through the dense forest until they reached the spring she had mentioned. The water was clear and sparkling, and they eagerly drank from it, savoring the refreshing taste. True to Angel's words, as soon as they drank, the hidden path that had once been obscured emerged before them, clearly marking their way forward.

Feeling a wave of relief wash over them, the group decided to take a well-deserved break. They settled around the spring, enjoying the serene atmosphere and the cool shade provided by the surrounding trees. The fresh fruits from the nearby trees proved to be delicious and revitalizing. Their hunger was satiated, and they filled their bags with as much fruit as they could carry for the journey ahead.

As they rested, the peaceful surroundings allowed them to regain their energy and reflect on their progress. The spring not only provided physical nourishment but also renewed their spirits and strengthened their resolve for the challenges that lay ahead.

With their bellies full and their bags stocked, the group was ready to continue their adventure, now guided by the trail once again.

CHAPTER SEVENTEEN

STORY OF SELENE

As the team rejuvenated and prepared for their journey, Angel approached them with a serious expression.

"From your conversations, I've realized that the world I left behind is no longer the world I will be returning to. It has changed significantly since I was transformed and stuck here. However, despite this, I still want to go back and start a new life. The forest holds too many bad memories for me to stay," Angel said, her voice steady but filled with emotion. "If you'll allow me, I would like to join your journey."

Her eyes searched theirs for acceptance, hoping they would understand her desire for a fresh start and the need to leave the forest behind.

Mira looked at Angel with a reassuring smile. "What are you talking about, Angel? You're already part of our team. We wouldn't have made it this far without you."

Angel's eyes brightened with gratitude, a hint of relief softening her features. "Thank you, Mira. It means a lot to hear that."

Elena chimed in, "Absolutely. We're stronger together, and your knowledge of the forest and its secrets is invaluable. We're all in this together now."

Magnus nodded in agreement. "Your presence has already made a difference. We're glad to have you with us, and we'll face whatever challenges come our way as a united group."

As the team continued along the newly revealed path, Magnus's curiosity got the better of him. He turned to Angel, and asked, "So, Angel, what's your story? How did you manage to get this far into the forest? In all my years as a Guardian, no one has ever crossed the Pink River. How did you make it this far?"

Angel glanced at Magnus, her expression a mix of sadness and determination. "It's a long story, but I'll share it with you."

Angel took a deep breath, her eyes reflecting the depth of her past experiences. "Many years ago, I lived in Nocturna with my father. My father was a fisherman, so I grew up around water sources. One day, soldiers came to our village and announced that anyone interested in making some extra money and seeking adventure should gather at the palace. My friends and I decided to take the opportunity."

She paused, a wistful look in her eyes. "At the palace, we learned that the King needed something from the forest. He wanted us to retrieve an object held by a mysterious lady deep within the cave. In return, we would be handsomely rewarded."

Angel's voice grew softer, tinged with regret. "We were unaware of the dangers that lay ahead. Drawn by curiosity and the allure of the forest's mysteries, we ventured into it. I had heard tales about the Pink River and its enchantments. Among my people, the story of a pink river and the magical fishes that resided in it was famous. These fishes were said to produce a bountiful catch every day."

"Even I have heard the tale of the pink fish," Magnus nodded in agreement. "It's a legend that has intrigued many."

She looked down, tears welling in her eyes and continued. "I thought that if I could bring back one of those magical fishes, it would relieve my father of his daily struggle to catch enough fish for us to survive. But I never imagined that my journey would lead me to be trapped here, transformed and separated from everything I knew."

Tears started to slide down her cheek as she continued, her voice trembling. "I left my old father all alone, and all these years, I've been trying to find a way back. My heart aches knowing that I've missed so much and that I would never be able to make things right."

Mira, moved by Angel's story, placed a comforting hand on her shoulder.

Angel continued, her voice heavy with the weight of her memories. "Once we reached the forest, one by one, people started disappearing. It was as if the forest itself was pulling them away. We were terrified and disoriented, unsure of what to do or how to go back. Only a few of us remained."

She paused, a deep sadness clouding her eyes. "In a desperate attempt to continue, we built a boat to cross the Pink River. The river was beautiful but treacherous, and as we ventured into its waters, the currents of the once peaceful looking river became increasingly violent. It felt as though the river itself was fighting against us. Despite our efforts, the boat was overwhelmed. One by one, everyone was washed away by the force of the current."

Angel's voice trembled as she recounted the ordeal. "I jumped out of the boat, determined not to succumb to the river's wrath. I swam with all my strength, fighting against the roaring current. Somehow, I managed to reach the shore. Exhausted and alone, I crawled onto the riverbank, barely clinging to consciousness."

She looked at her companions, her expression a mixture of sorrow and resolve. "The forest had claimed my friends, and I was left stranded, facing the unknown. With no other choice, I ventured further into the forest, driven by the hope of finding the object we were sent for and a way to escape."

By the time I reached that tree with purple fruit, I was very hungry, just like Xavier I ended up eating the fruit.

Elena's eyes softened with sympathy. "It must have been incredibly hard to endure such loss and isolation."

Angel nodded, her gaze distant. "It was. But that hardship made me more determined. I kept searching, driven by the memory of my friends and the hope of returning to my father. Even when I was transformed and trapped, I never gave up on the idea of finding a way back."

Angel continued, her voice steady despite the weight of her memories. "Recently, I saw the witch heading towards the other side of the forest. Driven by desperation and curiosity, I followed her. She made her way to the hidden window that led into the well. I watched as she descended into it, but after a while, she vanished without a trace."

She glanced at the group, her eyes reflecting both relief and lingering tension. "While heading back, I was suddenly attacked by a snake. If you hadn't intervened and saved me, I don't know what would have happened."

Magnus, moved by her story, placed a reassuring hand on her shoulder. "Your bravery and perseverance are commendable. We'll face the challenges ahead together, and we'll make sure your journey ends in success."

At that moment, Elena, Mira, and Xavier exchanged worried glances. The question on their minds was clear: Did the witch know about their presence in the forest?

CHAPTER EIGHTEEN

A SANCTUARY FOR MAGICAL BEINGS

As the group approached the base of the mountain, they were greeted by a diverse array of animals they had never encountered before. Elena, Mira, and Xavier gazed in awe at the strange and wondrous creatures. "Look at these animals!" Elena exclaimed, her eyes wide with amazement. "I've seen similar ones in the cave paintings we discovered. We thought they were just mythical beings. It's incredible to see that many of the forest's animals actually live here."

Mira, ever cautious, kept her whistle within easy reach, prepared to use it if any of the animals exhibited aggressive behavior. Her fingers rested on the tail of the bird shaped whistle, ready to act at a moment's notice.

"Do you see that one?" Mira asked, pointing at a particularly unusual creature with an elongated body and iridescent scales that shimmered in the sunlight. "I had a nightmare about a creature like that in the hidden room. It looked menacing in my dream, but here it seems oddly harmless."

Magnus, who had been quietly observing the animals, nodded in understanding. "That's a 'Visorite.' Despite its eerie appearance with its tall, slender frame and a single, unblinking eye it's actually harmless. The legends say that these creatures, though they look unsettling, possess no malice."

He continued, his tone taking on a more reflective quality, "In ancient times, there were many tales about these beings. People believed they had a unique magical power. It was said that with just a touch, a Visorite could make someone's deepest desire come true.

Magnus's gaze grew distant, as if lost in thought. "However, before the Onyx Panther dynasty came to power, these magical beings began to disappear. It wasn't just the Visorites; many extraordinary creatures with mystical abilities vanished from our world. Some scholars believe their disappearance is tied to the rise of new powers and shifts in the balance of magic. Legends speak of a time when these creatures roamed freely, their magic intertwined with the very fabric of our world. Now, their stories are little more than whispers on the wind, remnants of a bygone era."

Elena, intrigued by Magnus's words, asked, "How did these animals come to be here? Have you seen any of them in your kingdom before?"

Magnus shook his head thoughtfully, his brow furrowing in contemplation. "No, I haven't encountered these creatures in my kingdom. They're entirely new to me. I only started seeing them after I arrived in this forest. It's as if this forest is a sanctuary for them, a hidden refuge that I wasn't aware of before coming to this forest."

He looked around at the diverse wildlife with a mixture of wonder and concern. "This forest seems to hold many secrets, and these animals are just one facet of them. Their sudden appearance might be linked to the forest's ancient magic or its hidden history."

As the group reached the base of the mountain, Xavier took a moment to survey the path leading upward. "It looks like the trail continues up the mountain," he observed, noting the rugged terrain that lay ahead. "We'll need to prepare ourselves for the climb."

Angel, her expression serious, added a note of caution. "The witch lives in these mountains. We need to be extremely careful and avoid making any noise. Her presence is a significant danger, and any disturbance might attract unwanted attention."

The group nodded in agreement, their earlier excitement now tempered by the realization of the challenge that lay ahead. They gathered their gear, ensuring they were adequately prepared for the ascent, and began their cautious climb up the mountain.

As the sun began to set and the sky turned to shades of pink and orange, the moon started to rise, casting a silvery glow over the landscape. Mira and Elena pointed toward the sky, their faces reflecting a mix of awe and concern.

"Look!" Mira urged. "The moon is nearly full. We need to act before it's fully illuminated."

The realization that a full moon might bring additional dangers spurred the group into action. With a shared understanding of the urgency, they decided to press on through the encroaching darkness.

As they continued their climb, a majestic stag appeared before them, its body emitting a soft, ethereal glow. "Look!" Elena exclaimed, her eyes widening in amazement. "Isn't that the same stag we saw in the hidden room?"

"It looks like it," Mira replied, her voice filled with wonder and relief.

The stag approached them calmly, nuzzling Mira gently before starting to lead the way. "The light from the stag is illuminating the path," Xavier observed. "We can continue trekking even in the dark now."

With the path illuminated by the stag's gentle glow, the team pressed forward with renewed energy and determination. The moonlight cast long shadows, and the soft light from the stag created an almost magical atmosphere as they climbed.

As they ascended further, the path led them to a large boulder that seemed to block their way. The trail appeared to pass through it, but the boulder was imposing and seemed to challenge their progress. The team halted, uncertain of how to proceed.

Angel stepped forward and examined the boulder closely. "This is the entrance to the witch's lair," she said with a note of finality. "We've reached her dwelling."

The realization of their proximity to their goal made the group pause and reconsider their approach. They needed a solid plan to confront the witch and navigate the challenges that lay ahead. They gathered around the boulder, discussing their strategy and brainstorming ideas on how best to proceed.

Magnus spoke up, breaking the silence. "We should stay here tonight. Given the danger of this place, it's crucial that we maintain vigilance. At least one person must always be on watch."

He continued, "Let's take turns staying awake. Two people can keep the watch at a time while the others rest. This way, we can keep each other awake."

The group agreed with Magnus's plan, understanding the importance of maintaining vigilance in such a perilous environment. They quickly organized a watch schedule, assigning roles for the night. With their strategy in place, they prepared for a long night ahead, knowing that the success of their mission depended on their careful planning and execution.

As the night deepened, the team took their positions. The soft, eerie glow of the moon cast an otherworldly light over the mountain, and the occasional rustle of leaves or distant animal call added to the sense of anticipation. The group remained focused, their minds racing with thoughts of the confrontation that awaited them.

Each member of the team knew that tomorrow would bring new challenges, and they were determined to face them with courage and resolve. As they settled into their roles, they took solace in their camaraderie and the shared purpose that had brought them to this moment.

In the quiet of the night, with the moon casting its silver light over the rugged terrain, the team prepared themselves for the crucial steps that would follow. Their resolve was unshakable, and their readiness to face the witch and overcome the obstacles in their path was unwavering.

The following morning, the team assembled to finalize their strategy. With the full moon looming later that night, they were acutely aware of the tight window of opportunity they had. Angel, drawing from her knowledge of the witch's habits, addressed the group.

"The witch leaves her lair and ventures into the forest every full moon night," Angel said firmly. "We're certain of this. It's our chance to act. Once she departs, we must move swiftly."

The plan was straightforward, they would wait for the full moon to rise. As twilight gave way to night and the moon ascended into the sky, the team would set their plan into motion. Elena, Mira, and Xavier were tasked with creating a diversion. Their objective was to find a way to distract the animals that guarded the witch's lair. This required not only careful planning but also inventive thinking to ensure the animals were either drawn away or kept occupied, thus clearing the path to the entrance.

Meanwhile, Angel and Magnus would take advantage of the resulting chaos to infiltrate the witch's house. Stealth was paramount; they needed to slip inside undetected and carry out their objectives with precision. Their mission was to complete whatever was necessary to advance and secure a way out of the witch's domain.

"Once we're inside, our actions must be both quick and efficient," Angel stressed. "We won't have much time before the witch returns. Every second will count."

Throughout the day, the team made their final preparations. They meticulously reviewed their roles and contingency plans, ensuring that everyone was clear on their responsibilities. As the moon began its ascent, casting a silvery glow over the landscape, they braced themselves for the critical night ahead.

CHAPTER NINETEEN

THE WITCH'S LAIR

True to her routine, the witch emerged as the full moon reached its zenith. Her lair was guarded by a vigilant array of animals, each one stationed meticulously around the cave entrance

As the witch mounted her horse and rode off into the forest, the creatures maintained their watchful positions, their eyes glinting in the moonlight.

Seizing the opportunity, the team jumped into action. Mira quickly took out her whistle and blew a loud, sharp call. A flock of birds appeared and swooped down towards the animals at the entrance of the cave. Mira gave clear commands, directing the birds to attack. The birds flurried around, pecking and flapping their wings, causing a chaotic scene as the animals tried to escape.

Amidst the commotion, the team moved swiftly and silently. They slipped through the chaos and into the witch's lair, their movements careful and deliberate to avoid drawing any attention. As the birds continued their disruption outside, the group took their first steps into the heart of the witch's house, their footsteps echoing softly on the cold, stone floor, ready to carry out their plan before the witch's return.

The interior of the lair was dimly lit by flickering torches and the ethereal light of the full moon filtering through narrow windows. The air was thick with the smell of herbs and magic, and strange artifacts were scattered around—potions, scrolls, and ancient books lined the shelves.

Suddenly, a small creature began bouncing energetically in front of them. It was a captivating sight: a creature about the size of a cat, with plush, velvety fur that shimmered softly in the dim light.

Mira's eyes widened with delight. "Look, a rabbit!!"

Angel shook her head, a knowing smile on her lips. "It's not a rabbit. It's called a Puffernabbit."

The Puffernabbit continued its lively hopping, its fur glowing faintly with a calming, pastel light. As it moved, tiny sparkles of light seemed to follow its every step, leaving a trail of gentle glitter in the air. Its large, expressive eyes, glowing with a warm amber hue, surveyed the newcomers with a curious and friendly gaze.

Angel continued, "The Puffernabbit is a charming, whimsical creature that closely resembles a rabbit but with a few enchanting twists. For instance, its fur has a soft, glow-in-the-dark quality that adds an ethereal touch to its presence. And its whiskers are enchanted—they can detect and respond to the emotions of those around it."

The Puffernabbit's whiskers twitched in response to Angel's words, and it bounded closer, seemingly sensing the group's curiosity. The creature's fur pulsed gently, its colors shifting with the ebb and flow of the moonlight streaming through the windows.

Mira crouched down, extending a hand towards the Puffernabbit. "It's adorable! I've never seen anything like it."

Angel nodded, watching the Puffernabbit's whiskers quiver slightly as it approached Mira. "It's a magical companion that brings a touch of wonder wherever it goes. It's known to provide comfort and joy, especially in places like this where the air is thick with magic."

The Puffernabbit, sensing the warmth in Mira's voice, nuzzled up to her hand, its tail swaying gently. The room seemed to brighten just a little as the creature's soft, glowing presence infused the dim space with a hint of enchantment.

"Look!!" Xavier exclaimed, pointing urgently at the trail before them. The path they had been following seemed to lead straight into the witch's lair and then abruptly ended at a solid stone wall.

The group gathered around the wall, their faces marked with frustration and concern. The barrier was thick and ancient, etched with mysterious symbols that emitted a faint, eerie glow. It was clear this was no ordinary wall—it was magically reinforced, designed to keep intruders at bay.

"We need to find a way through this wall, and fast," Angel said with a sense of urgency. "We can't afford to stay here any longer. The witch will be back soon."

Magnus glanced around the room, his eyes scanning the dimly lit interior for any potential clues or objects that might aid their predicament. His expression was thoughtful, a mix of frustration and determination. "This wall is enchanted with a powerful protective spell," he said, his voice carrying a note of urgency. "Breaking through it isn't an option. We need to find another solution."

The group quickly sprang into action, each member focusing on a different aspect of the room to uncover any hints or tools that could help them bypass the magical barrier. The atmosphere was tense but focused, as every second counted in their quest to find a way through the wall before the witch's return.

Angel and Magnus, recognizing the importance of magical knowledge, immediately began to sift through the array of books and scrolls scattered throughout the lair. She and Magnus worked in collaboration, flipping through pages and unrolling scrolls, searching for any spells or incantations that could counteract or neutralize the protective spell on the wall.

Meanwhile, Elena turned her attention to the potions and magical brews that lined the shelves. The shelves were cluttered with vials and bottles of varying sizes, each containing liquids of different colors and consistencies. The air was heavy with the scent of herbs and alchemical concoctions. Elena carefully examined each potion, looking for anything that might be related to opening hidden passages or dispelling magical barriers. She checked labels and inscriptions, hoping to find a potion that could aid in their current predicament.

Mira and Xavier, on the other hand, focused on searching for any mechanical or magical switches that could potentially open a secret passage or unlock a hidden entry point. They meticulously examined the walls, floors, and any ornate fixtures or carvings that might conceal a switch. Their movements were cautious but thorough, as they tapped on walls, tested the pressure of various stones, and scrutinized any unusual features in the room's architecture.

As the minutes ticked by, the team's efforts began to bear fruit. Angel's and Magnus's relentless investigation of the books and scrolls led them to a promising spell mentioned in an old, tattered manuscript. The spell, described in intricate detail, was designed to reveal hidden passages and bypass magical barriers when combined with the right ingredients.

Excited by their discovery, Angel shared the information with the rest of the group. "I think we've found something," she said, her voice filled with cautious optimism. "There's a spell that can reveal hidden passages. It requires a specific potion, and fortunately, we might have that here."

Elena, who had been examining the potions, nodded in agreement. "I found a vial labeled 'Essence of Revelation.' It sounds like it could be what we need. The potion might work in conjunction with the spell to reveal any hidden mechanisms behind the wall."

With renewed hope, Angel and Magnus carefully prepared the potion according to the spell's instructions. They mixed the Essence of Revelation with other ingredients mentioned in the manuscript, following each step with precision. The potion began to emit a faint, shimmering light as it was mixed, indicating that they were on the right track.

The team agreed to take a chance and try the solution on the wall.

Meanwhile Mira looked at an interesting book and slid it inside her bag.

The team prepared themselves as Magnus carefully uncorked the vial. He poured the shimmering liquid over the wall's surface, while reading the incantations on the manuscript . As the liquid touched the wall, it began to glow more intensely, and the mysterious symbols seemed to pulse with energy.

A door opened in the wall, the door expanded until it was large enough for the group to pass through. It revealed a rope bridge that seemed to sway with every breath of wind. Its worn planks creaked under the weight of unseen years, adding an eerie but intriguing sound to the scene. A shimmering, translucent portal gradually formed at the end of the bridge, glowing with the same iridescent light as the potion.

"It's working!" Elena said, her eyes wide with awe. "Let's go through before it wears off."

The team moved quickly towards the door on the wall.

Suddenly, a loud, unsettling noise echoed through the lair. The witch had returned, and the distant sound of her footsteps growing louder sent a jolt of panic through the group.

CHAPTER TWENTY

THE PORTAL

"Run!!" Magnus shouted, his voice echoing through the dimly lit lair. Panic surged through the team as they dashed towards the shimmering portal at the end of the swaying rope bridge. The urgency in Magnus's voice propelled them forward, but the bridge, burdened by the weight of the fleeing group, began to creak and sway violently.

The rope bridge, old and weathered, strained under the pressure. Each step the team took made the planks groan and wobble alarmingly. The once-steady bridge now moved like a pendulum, swinging back and forth with increasing intensity.

Behind them, the witch's furious scream pierced the air. "Do you think you can invade my home in my absence and escape unscathed?" Her voice, filled with dark magic, reverberated ominously through the cavern. With a wave of her hand, she began chanting a series of incantations. The air around the bridge crackled with dark energy, and the bridge's movement grew even more erratic.

The team pushed forward, their breaths coming in sharp, ragged gasps. The portal was almost within reach, its iridescent light casting a faint glow on their determined faces. Just as they neared the end of the bridge, a heart-stopping sight froze Mira in her tracks. The Puffernabbit, which had been following closely behind her, was teetering perilously on the edge of the swaying bridge.

The little creature's tiny paws scrabbled desperately at the uneven planks, its large, amber eyes wide with fear. Mira's heart clenched at the sight. She couldn't bear to see the Puffernabbit fall to its doom, even as the bridge swayed more violently under the witch's magical assault.

Without a second thought, Mira hurled herself back towards the Puffernabbit. The bridge swayed violently, and Mira struggled to maintain her balance as she crawled toward the creature. Her mind raced with the possibility of falling, but her resolve was unshakable. She extended her hand towards the Puffernabbit, which was now perilously close to slipping off.

With a final, desperate lunge, Mira managed to grab the Puffernabbit just as it was about to fall. She clutched the small creature tightly, her heart pounding in her chest. The Puffernabbit nuzzled against her hand, sensing her desperation and clinging to her for dear life.

The bridge creaked ominously as Mira struggled to get back to her feet, the witch's dark magic intensifying the bridge's violent swings. Mira's arms trembled under the weight of the Puffernabbit, but she gritted her teeth and fought against the fear clawing at her.

"Mira, come on!" Elena's voice rang out urgently from the portal, her outstretched hand beckoning Mira and the Puffernabbit towards safety.

But as she started to make her way back to the portal, the bridge swung wildly. Mira's path was obstructed by a sudden, blinding flash of light—an indication of the witch's power surging. The witch had cast a powerful spell, and a barrier of dark energy formed in front of the portal, making the escape even more perilous.

As she neared the portal, she felt a sudden, powerful force grip her. The witch's magic had reached out, ensnaring Mira in an invisible grasp. Mira struggled against the pull, but the witch's spell was too strong. She was lifted off her feet, and the magical force dragged her back towards the center of the bridge.

"No!" Elena's voice rang out in despair as she saw Mira being pulled away. "Mira, no!"

Despite the team's desperate cries, the witch's spell continued to pull Mira towards her. Mira's eyes locked with Elena's, and a look of sorrow passed between them.

With a last, determined push, Mira tried to fight the magical pull, but it was no use. The witch's dark magic enveloped her, and she was yanked away from the portal's edge, her cries swallowed by the howling winds of the bridge.

In a blinding flash of light, the portal closed, and Mira was left behind, trapped in the lair with the witch. The remaining members of the team, now safely on the other side of the portal, could only watch in horror as the portal sealed shut, cutting off their chance to rescue their friend.

The team stood in stunned silence, their relief at their own escape mingled with deep sorrow and worry for Mira. The urgency of their situation had taken a heartbreaking turn, and the weight of their loss was heavy.

"We need to get back!" Elena cried out, her voice trembling with a mix of fear and determination. Her eyes were wide with panic as she looked back at the now-closed portal. "I can't go home without Mira! How do I answer my parents?"

The gravity of their situation hit Elena with full force. Her sister, Mira, was trapped behind the sealed portal with the witch, and the thought of returning without her was unbearable. Tears welled up in Elena's eyes as she took a deep breath, her resolve hardening.

"I want to wait here," Elena continued, her voice breaking but resolute. "I'm not going back without Mira."

The team exchanged worried glances. They knew Elena's determination came from a place of deep love and loyalty, but the danger they faced was immense. The portal was now sealed shut, and the witch's dark magic was still strong. However, they also understood that leaving one of their own behind was not an option.

As Elena and the others frantically searched the lair for a way to reopen the portal, a profound silence fell over the cavern.

In the dim light of the lair, the witch's cold, stern expression softened as she had witnessed Mira's selflessness. She had been prepared to exact her revenge and secure her home from intruders, but the sight of Mira, clutching the Puffernabbit with unwavering determination and risking everything for a creature so small, stirred something deep within her.

The witch stepped out from the shadows, her imposing figure casting a long, eerie silhouette across the cavern. Her eyes, once filled with dark resolve, now reflected a flicker of something different—perhaps regret, or even compassion.

Mira, still trembling from her recent ordeal, looked up at the witch with wary eyes. Her heart pounded as she awaited whatever fate the witch might have in store for her.

The witch approached, her gaze fixed on Mira. "I have been watching," she began, her voice softer than before. "I saw what you did for the Puffernabbit. You risked everything to save a creature that means more to me than you could understand."

Mira's eyes widened in disbelief. She had expected the witch to remain implacable and unyielding, but the shift in her demeanor was undeniable.

"You showed bravery and kindness," the witch continued, her voice growing gentler. "Qualities that I had nearly forgotten. It was a gesture that touched me deeply."

With a wave of her hand, the witch dissolved the dark barrier that had sealed the portal. The shimmering portal reappeared, its light a beacon of hope for the team. The witch's eyes, though still tinged with the hardness of her years, now held a glimmer of warmth.

As the portal reopened, Elena and the rest of the team didn't hesitate. Driven by a mix of desperation and resolve, they sprinted back towards the lair, their hearts pounding with the hope of rescuing Mira.

The air was tense with anticipation as they crossed the swaying bridge and entered the dimly lit lair once more. The flickering torches cast long shadows on the cold stone walls, and the smell of herbs and magic filled their nostrils. Their eyes quickly scanned the cavern for any sign of Mira.

But what greeted them was the witch, who had moments earlier been a formidable figure of menace and dark power, now stood in the center of the lair with an air of surprising calm. Her stern demeanor had softened, replaced by a welcoming expression that was almost unrecognizable.

"You've returned," the witch said, her voice holding a note of genuine warmth. "And you bring with you a strength and compassion that has touched me deeply."

Elena and the others came to a halt, their expressions a mix of confusion and cautious hope. The witch's demeanor was a stark contrast to the hostile figure they had faced earlier.

The lair, once a place of treacherous magic, now seemed bathed in a softer, more inviting light.

"I have been reflecting on your bravery and selflessness," the witch continued, her gaze moving from one member of the team to the next. "You have shown me qualities that I had nearly forgotten. You risked everything for each other and for a creature that I hold dear."

Elena, her eyes wide with a mix of relief and disbelief, stepped forward. "Are you saying... you're going to help us?"

The witch nodded, a gentle smile touching her lips. "Indeed. I am impressed by your determination and kindness. You have proven yourselves worthy. As such, I will assist you in returning to your world and offer my aid in any way I can."

The team exchanged astonished looks. The witch's unexpected change of heart was as profound as it was bewildering.

"But... What about Mira?" Angel asked, her voice tinged with concern.

The witch's gaze softened further. "Mira is safe. She has shown great bravery, and for that, she will be treated with respect. I will not hold her captive. You may retrieve her and leave with my blessing."

But before that you must accept my hospitality.

CHAPTER TWENTY ONE

TALE OF THE WITCH

The witch raised her hand with a graceful wave, and a grand wooden table materialized in the center of the lair. Six intricately carved chairs appeared around it, each adorned with elegant curves and mystical symbols. She instructed everyone to take a seat.

A chaos erupted in the previously calm kitchen. Knives danced through the air, slicing through a colorful array of fruits and vegetables with precise, rhythmic motions. The vibrant produce was chopped and diced with remarkable speed, creating a medley of textures and colors.

Spatulas and ladles whirled about, stirring and mixing ingredients in an assortment of pots and pans that had also appeared on the table. Steam began to rise from the cooking vessels, carrying with it the tantalizing aroma of herbs and spices blending together.

The once ominous lair was now filled with the rich, inviting scent of a sumptuous feast. The witch, her stern expression now softened by a hint of warmth, observed the scene with a sense of satisfaction. The air was filled with the sounds of cooking—sizzling, bubbling, and the occasional clatter of utensils—creating a cozy, almost homey atmosphere amidst the cavern's ancient stone walls.

The team watched in awe as the magical preparation unfolded before them. The enchanting transformation of the lair, once a place of danger and darkness, now radiated with the promise of comfort and hospitality. The aroma of the meal, rich and appetizing, filled their senses, offering a welcome reprieve from the tension and fear that had gripped them moments earlier.

As the table was set and the meal neared completion, the team exchanged looks of disbelief and cautious relief. The witch's unexpected gesture of hospitality, paired with the promise of help, signaled a remarkable shift in their dire situation.

Mira, summoning her courage, addressed the witch. "How should we address you, Miss?"

The witch, now revealed as Agatha, began to speak. "My name is Agatha. I have been observing you all this time. When I discovered that the cave, which had been peaceful for centuries, had been disturbed, I was initially furious. But when I arrived and saw who had entered, I was stunned to find only a group of young people, and I was also curious."

Agatha's gaze softened as she continued. "I decided to let you follow your own path, allowing fate to play out without my interference. Yet, as I watched, I saw that you were not only clever but also kind-hearted. You managed to complete your journey, and in doing so, helped Selene and Magnus as well."

Angel and Magnus nodded in agreement. "Their presence of mind has freed us, and we are forever grateful," Angel said, her voice filled with sincerity.

As Agatha's words settled in, the aroma of the freshly prepared feast drew everyone's attention. The grand wooden table, now adorned with an array of delicious dishes, was a sight to behold. The food was an exquisite display of colors and textures, with steaming pots of hearty stews, fresh salads, and an assortment of baked goods.

The team, their exhaustion momentarily forgotten, eagerly took their seats around the table. They served themselves heaping portions of the mouthwatering meal, savoring each bite as if they had never tasted anything like it before. The flavors were rich and complex, a testament to the skill and magic of Agatha's cooking.

Laughter and conversation flowed freely as they enjoyed the feast. The once-foreboding lair was now filled with the comforting sounds of camaraderie and contentment. Agatha, observing the scene with a hint of satisfaction, seemed to revel in the transformation of her lair from a place of peril to one of warmth and hospitality.

Xavier, now feeling more comfortable in Agatha's presence, ventured to ask, "Agatha, why are you living here all alone?"

Agatha's expression grew contemplative as she considered the question. She took a deep breath, and for a moment, the weight of her solitude seemed to hang in the air.

"This cave has been my sanctuary for many years," she began, her voice carrying a hint of nostalgia. "I chose this place long ago as a retreat from the outside world. It offered me solitude and a space to practice my magic in peace. Over the centuries, I have grown accustomed to this isolation, finding solace in my work and the creatures I care for."

Her gaze drifted to the Puffernabbit, which was now nestled comfortably on the table, content and safe. "The Puffernabbit, for example, has been my companion for as long as I can remember and its presence has been a source of comfort and connection for me."

"I was once a princess of the greatest kingdom," she began, her voice carrying the weight of distant memories. "Our kingdom was a land of magic and harmony, where people and magical creatures coexisted in peace. The animals were not just companions; they were integral to our way of life, and their well-being ensured that our people lived happily and prosperously."

Agatha's eyes grew distant, reflecting on the past. "But everything changed when the Onyx Panther dynasty, from a neighboring kingdom, attacked us. Their aim was to harm our magical creatures and destroy the delicate balance we had with nature. The war was devastating. We fought fiercely, but ultimately, we lost. Our kingdom was left in ruins, and we had no survivors left except for my father, myself, and the court sorcerer."

Agatha's tone grew somber as she continued. "In the aftermath, unsure of what to do and with our world in tatters, our sorcerer gathered all his remaining energy and created this sanctuary. This place was meant to be a haven for the magical creatures, a refuge from those who sought to destroy them. My father stayed behind to guard the entrance to the cave, ensuring that no one could harm us in the process of safeguarding the animals. We used a magical whistle to gather all the creatures and guide them here."

A shadow of grief passed over her face. "Tragically, my father was killed in the attack. We managed to seal the door behind us, protecting the sanctuary and the remaining magical creatures from those who would do them harm.

Agatha's gaze softened as she spoke of the past. "I came here with the sorcerer, who taught me everything he knew about magic. After a few years, he passed away, leaving me to continue his work. I chose to remain here, not only to protect the sanctuary but also to experiment with magic in peace. It became a safe place for the animals and for me, a place where I could carry on his legacy and preserve the magic that once thrived in our kingdom."

The team listened in rapt silence, moved by Agatha's story. The witch's solitude, once shrouded in mystery and fear, now revealed itself as a testament to loss, duty, and enduring commitment.

"I suppose," Agatha concluded, a touch of melancholy in her voice, "that in my quest to protect and preserve, I have also remained isolated, perhaps more than I intended. But seeing you all, and witnessing your bravery and kindness, has reminded me of the world beyond these walls."

The room was filled with a reflective quiet as Agatha's words sank in. The team, now understanding the depth of Agatha's past and the reasons for her solitude, felt a renewed sense of connection and respect for the witch who had once seemed so formidable.

CHAPTER TWENTY TWO

THE WAY BACK HOME

As the team prepared to depart, their minds still reeling from the evening's revelations, Agatha approached with a gentle smile. She held a small, intricately carved wooden box in her hands and walked over to Mira, offering it with a graceful nod.

"This is for you," Agatha said, her voice imbued with warmth and a sense of finality. "It's a token of our time together. May it serve you well."

Mira opened the box to reveal a stunning amulet, shimmering softly on a bed of velvet. Shaped like a crescent moon, its surface was adorned with delicate, swirling runes that seemed to come alive in the dim light of the lair.

"This amulet contains a fragment of the magic that sustains this place," Agatha explained. At that moment, Mira remembered the whistle she had found and handed it back to Agatha. "This must belong to you," she said.

Agatha's gaze shifted to Magnus. From within her robe, she drew forth a gleaming, ornate horn. Its surface was engraved with ancient runes and intricate designs, and it radiated a faint, pulsating glow.

"This," Agatha said, handing the horn to Magnus, "is the Horn of Command. It has the power to summon and control forces from afar. When you blow this horn, it will call forth a legion of magical soldiers to aid you in battle. Use it wisely, for it can turn the tide in the fiercest of confrontations and you shall use it once only."

Magnus took the horn, feeling its power and weight in his hands. The promise of summoning a magical army filled him with a sense of responsibility and anticipation.

The team shared appreciative glances, deeply moved by Agatha's gifts. Mira held the amulet close, feeling its warmth and the faint hum of its magic, while Magnus examined the Horn of Command, contemplating the strategic advantage it could provide.

With a final, graceful wave of her hand, Agatha conjured a swirling, radiant portal that shimmered with a spectrum of colors. The portal hovered in the air, casting a soft, ethereal light that gently illuminated the cavern's walls.

Then she said, "You will return to where you began. This portal will take you back to the entrance of the cave, where your journey first started. May your future be filled with wonder and success. farewell"

The team gathered around the portal, their hearts a mix of excitement and wistfulness. As they prepared to step through, Agatha's figure grew smaller in the distance, her presence a poignant reminder of the adventure's end.

With one last, lingering look at Agatha, the team stepped into the portal. The familiar sensation of being transported enveloped them as the swirling colors surrounded them. As the world shifted, they knew they were returning to their starting point, forever transformed by their extraordinary encounter with the witch who had offered them new insights into magic and bravery.

The team tumbled onto the ground with a jarring force. To their astonishment, they found themselves back at the same wall that had originally drawn them inside. Panic set in as they quickly realized that Angel and Magnus were missing.

Their concern grew until they heard faint calls of their names. They sprinted towards the source of the voices and were relieved to find Ms. Sumaya waiting for them. They rushed to her, beginning to apologize for their unexpected absence, but Ms. Sumaya cut them off.

"I told you not to fall behind," she said, her tone a mix of exasperation and relief. "Come on, everyone is looking for you."

The trio exchanged bewildered glances, their confusion evident.

As the team joined the rest of the class, it quickly became apparent that they hadn't just returned to the same place but also to the same time. The familiar surroundings and the voices they heard were all indicative of moments they had just experienced, but everything was exactly as it had been before they ventured into the cave.

Their realization dawned on them simultaneously—this wasn't just a return to the physical location but a rewind to the exact moment before their disappearance. The sense of déjà vu was undeniable, and the events that had just transpired now seemed like they had been replayed.

Their bewilderment deepened as they looked at each other, trying to piece together what had just happened. The mystery of Angel and Magnus's absence lingered, but the understanding that they had somehow looped back in time added a new layer of complexity to their situation.

As the school trip concluded and the rest of the class discussed their experiences in the cave, Elena, Mira, and Xavier remained lost in thought, grappling with whether what had happened was real or merely a figment of their imagination.

CHAPTER TWENTY THREE

THE CONCLUSION

As the trio returned home, they wrestled with the dilemma of whether to share their extraordinary experiences with their parents. At dinner, Elena and Mira's mother, Maya, mentioned casually that she had stumbled upon a fascinating book about the archaeological site. She planned to write a story about it the following day.

Intrigued and eager for clarity, the trio decided to visit the local library the next morning to investigate the book further. They spent hours immersed in its pages, discovering that it chronicled the lives and deeds of King Magnus Ravenswood and Queen Selene Pinkfish. According to the book, these legendary monarchs had once sealed the very place they had just visited, a location fraught with mystery and danger, to prevent the disappearances that had once troubled their kingdom. The text made it clear that the seal was intended to remain unbroken forever, ensuring that the evil contained within would never escape.

Elena remarked, "It seems Magnus and Angel ensured the enchanted forest remained undisturbed by sealing the cave and weaving tales of evil to guard it. And we never knew Angel had the same last name as ours. Do you think it's a mere coincidence or somehow we are related to her..?"

Among the illustrations in the book, they found a striking drawing of Magnus and Angel. The two figures were depicted holding hands and smiling warmly, their expressions filled with a sense of peace and accomplishment. This illustration resonated deeply with the trio, evoking memories of their own encounters.

As they delved deeper into the book, the connections between their own experiences and the historical accounts became increasingly evident. Just as they had returned to their own time, Magnus and Angel must have also been sent back to theirs.

The book described how Magnus and Angel, armed with the powerful Horn of Command given by Agatha, had played a pivotal role in defeating the malevolent King Aric of Onyx Panther Dynasty. This horn, capable of summoning and controlling magical forces, had turned the tide in their battle, allowing them to secure the kingdom.

The realization of their role in these historical events was profound. The trio had unwittingly participated in a significant chapter of the kingdom's history, contributing to the defeat of a great evil and the preservation of peace. The understanding that they had helped shape and safeguard the future of the enchanting sanctuary, albeit from the shadows, brought them a deep sense of accomplishment and closure.

As they closed the book, the trio shared a reflective moment. What had begun as a seemingly simple school trip had turned into a crucial adventure that ensured the downfall of the wicked Onyx Panther Dynasty and emergence of Ravenswood dynasty, where people lived with safety and harmony.

Mira and Elena exchanged smiles, and as they did, the amulet around Mira's neck began to twinkle softly, a gentle reminder of their extraordinary journey and the magic that still lingered from their adventure.

9 798889 588096 8